WITHDRAWN

HERO
WORSHIP

For Steve Mitchell, who has made me a better writer
and—more importantly—a better person.

HERO
WORSHIP

CHRISTOPHER E. LONG

Woodbury, Minnesota

First Edition
Second Printing, 2014

Book design by Bob Gaul
Cover design by Kevin R. Brown
Cover illustration by Aaron Goodman
Cover image © iStock.com/8174944/Nikada

Flux, an imprint of Llewellyn Worldwide Ltd.

Library of Congress Cataloging-in-Publication Data
Long, Christopher E.
  Hero worship/Christopher E. Long.—First edition.
      pages cm
Summary: "When homeless teenager Marvin realizes his dream of working for the Core, an elite squad of costumed heroes, he discovers that the superstars he's idolized for so long aren't the people he thought they were"—Provided by publisher.
  ISBN 978-0-7387-3909-0
[1. Superheroes—Fiction. 2. Ability—Fiction. 3. Good and evil—Fiction. 4. Heroes—Fiction. 5. Friendship—Fiction. 6. Homeless persons—Fiction.]
I. Title.
  PZ7.L8445Her 2014
  [Fic]—dc23

                                        2013032700

                                    Flux
                        Llewellyn Worldwide Ltd.
                          2143 Wooddale Drive
                        Woodbury, MN 55125-2989
                            www.fluxnow.com

                  Printed in the United States of America

Acknowledgments

First off, with Scott Treimel, I've got the best agent on the planet. Then there's John M. Cusick, who helped shape *Hero Worship* with his guidance. I want to thank Mike and Lisa Kane for always being willing to read my work. And to everyone at Flux—Brian Farrey-Latz, Sandy Sullivan, and Mallory Hayes—you have made this process enjoyable for this rookie Young Adult writer.

Mom and Dad, you get your own paragraph—that's how important you are. Thanks for believing in me when I didn't believe in myself.

There are folks who helped me find my way with my comic book career who are equally responsible for this novel. Danny Miki encouraged me in the very beginning, and both Ted Adams and Jeff Mariotte gave me my first big break as a comic book writer. Working with Jim Valentino was a boot camp for what works and what doesn't work in the comic book medium. Axel Alonso gave me my shot at the majors. And Shannon Eric Denton has made sure I get published more than anyone else.

To my wife Jamie and son Jackson, there probably are words I could use to convey how important you are to me, but I'm just not that great a writer.

ONE

The sports car takes the corner clocking 60 mph, the back tires squealing and kicking up black smoke. The vehicle fishtails, and the rear bumper slams into a traffic-light post. But the tires never stop spinning, clawing onward like a hunted animal frantically trying to escape death. Then the car lurches forward through the afternoon traffic, zigging and zagging past delivery vans and taxis, barreling through a red light. It clips a city bus and swerves hard left, drifting across the blacktop toward the entrance to the city park.

Sitting on a park bench, a half-eaten hot dog raised to my mouth, I watch as the car crashes through the cast-iron gate and careens into the park. Joggers and rollerbladers scramble out of the way as it races down the pebble-covered path, spitting up tiny white rocks like the wake behind a speedboat.

"Are you guys seeing this?" I ask.

Kent is eating his hot dog like a python devouring a small animal. He looks up, just now becoming aware of the commotion. Kent looks like one of those obese people who've lost a lot of weight, which is good—but now have a thick layer of loose, floppy skin, which is bad.

"What's the freaking hurry?" he says, watching the erratic car.

On the other side of me, Yvonne shades her eyes to see the unfolding events. "Is someone chasing him?" she asks.

Shaking my head, I say, "Not that I can—"

A sonic boom rips through the air, shattering the windows of nearby storefronts and vehicles. Yvonne groans as she's knocked against the back of the bench, and Kent's baggy skin flaps like a flag in the wind. Cupping my hands over my ears, I grimace from the piercing shockwave.

A red blur shoots across the park and comes to a sudden stop directly in front of the speeding car. Even from a distance, I know who it is—the fastest thing on two legs.

"Hey, it's Streak!" I shout, immediately wishing I didn't sound so excited.

Yvonne dusts herself off. "Yippee, Marvin."

"I've never seen a member of the Core in person before," I say, angling to get a better view.

I possess an extensive collection of Core memorabilia, and there's one Streak item I'm particularly proud of. It's a commemorative action figure with multiple points of articulation and a base that prominently displays the Core insignia. Very rare and hard to come by.

Trust me here. Seeing Streak in action is way better!

Streak stands still as a statue as the car heads right for him. His recognizable red costume almost looks crimson, like blood. The glare from the sun makes it impossible from my angle to see who's behind the wheel of the car, but whoever it is pushes down on the accelerator, squeezing every drop out of the engine as 3,000 pounds of metal hurtles right at Streak. The car moves closer, closing the distance, until—

In the time it takes to blink, Streak is gone. The car, missing its intended target, speeds over an embankment and launches into the air. It lands with a crash, and sparks fly as the undercarriage scrapes across the concrete walkway. Momentarily losing control, the vehicle bounds toward the hot-dog stand where, just moments before, my friends and I purchased our lunch. A look of terror spreads across the vendor's face as he comes face-to-face with the car's grille.

Streak appears out of nowhere, grabs the vendor, and flings him into the air, out of harm's way. Right as the car strikes the cart, Streak is gone. The hot-dog vendor lands on the ground, skidding to a stop right at my feet. The speeding car runs into a large tree, abruptly ending the high-speed getaway. Smoke rises out of the crumpled metal.

"The cops won't be far behind," Yvonne mutters, slipping on a pair of sunglasses.

Stunned, the hot-dog vendor looks up at me, confusion stamped on his face.

"Are you okay?" I ask.

The man pushes himself up, but immediately drops back on the ground and howls in agony. "My arm!" he screams. The bone in his right arm is broken and sticking through the skin.

Kneeling down next to him, I say, "Yvonne, give him a hit."

"Yeah, okay," she says, bending down and placing a hand on the man's forehead. "I usually charge for this, but, under the circumstances, this one's on the house." Her eyes roll back in their sockets, revealing solid white orbs.

"ARGH! Argh … argh," the man moans. His facial features soften, and his frantic breathing slows considerably as he inhales deeply. Yvonne's eyes roll back down and she blinks a couple of times, rubbing the side of her head. The hot-dog vendor's eyes are glassy and unfocused. He gives us a crooked smile.

A red blur zips over to the wrecked car, and Streak peers inside the window. He turns around and stares in our direction. Before I have time to process whether or not he's looking at us, Streak appears right in front of me, stirring up leaves and a cloud of dust. He glances down at the hot-dog vendor. "Is he okay?" he asks.

I can only imagine how stupid I look with this cheesy grin on my face, but I don't really care. I'm completely geeked out and beside myself. He's so close, I could reach out and touch him. I actually consider doing this, but let's face it, that would be creepy.

"His arm's busted," Yvonne says.

The wounded man smiles at Streak and says, "I'm good. Gooooood. Goods."

Streak turns to me. "This man is on drugs."

The vendor lifts his broken arm, which is dripping blood from the gash, and points at Yvonne. "She toucheded me. Shhhhe'sss one of yous." He notices the bone protruding through the skin on his arm. "Oh, man, thisss ain't good."

"Is that so?" Streak asks. But before Yvonne can answer, he does a double take at Kent. "What the—"

The entire left side of Kent's face looks like melted

wax. A large slab of flesh hangs from his head. "Kent, your face," I whisper.

He feels his face and chuckles, saying, "Sorry." He cups the hanging flesh and molds it back into shape.

"Who are you?" Streak demands.

Kent, Yvonne, and I all look at each other, waiting for someone to say something, anything.

"You kids are dirty," Streak says.

"Kids?" Yvonne says. "I'm eighteen."

Streak zips over and grabs her arm so hard that she yelps. "In that case, you'll be tried under the Clean Powers Act as an adult," he says. His mouth opens as if he's going to say something more, but he only croaks. His eyes flutter repeatedly and he releases his grip on Yvonne, staggering back on wobbly legs before collapsing on the ground.

Yvonne's eyes go from solid white to normal. "Let's go," she says, hurrying off into the park. Kent follows behind her, doing his best to hold his face together.

Streak lies on the ground in a heap. His chest rises and falls.

"Streak's a hero," the hot-dog vendor says.

I struggle to find the words, but give up and turn to run after my friends. Yvonne and Kent make their way toward the subway. Pedestrians gawk at Kent's melting face as he passes. He flips the hood of his jacket over his head to conceal his disfigurement.

Catching up with Yvonne, I say, "Why'd you zap him?"

"Marvin, I didn't see you coming up with anything."

"But he's Streak. A member of the Core. You can't zap him."

"He said we were dirty."

"We are dirty," I say.

She gives me a patronizing look, like a mother would a child. "Well, yeah, but he doesn't know that for sure. He jumped to a conclusion, and based on what? How we look?"

"Hey you two, if you don't mind," Kent says, his flesh squishing through his fingers as he cups his face. "I'm turning into pudding here. Chop-chop."

The three of us hurry to the subway platform and manage to get onto the train just as the doors close. Luckily for us, everybody who rides the subways in Loganstin City takes great pains to avoid looking at the other passengers. If we're lucky, we'll get to our stop before Kent melts into a puddle in his seat.

TWO

I was homeless and living on the streets when I met Yvonne. She was the first person I'd ever encountered with powers. I spent three nights watching her in an alley behind a Fast Mart. Drug addicts would approach her and hand over some crumpled bills, and she'd lay a hand on their heads. It only took a few moments, but the effect of her power was evident by the sudden relaxed and serene expressions that appeared on her customers' faces. They would stumble away, only to return the next night.

It didn't take long for her to spot me watching. For some reason, I felt I could trust her. Maybe it was because she too didn't go through the Power Aversion Program. I told her my story—what I was capable of—and was impressed that she didn't flinch. She admitted to having a power that allowed her to ease another person's pain. In helping the junkies, Yvonne was doing what she had to do for survival, despite the fact that she was breaking the law. Living on the streets has opened my eyes to the reality of just how many dirties use their powers to make money. I might be the only one who doesn't.

I came back to the alley the next couple of nights, and Yvonne asked me where I was staying. I told her on a bench in Reese Park. She said there was plenty of space at her place, and she smiled when she said that it was conveniently located right by the freeway. She'd made a home inside the embankment of the Edinger Avenue overpass. She called it her concrete cave. It was built so safety inspectors could enter and check the bridge for structural damage. Thankfully there hadn't been any earthquakes in a few years, so no one had a reason to inspect the place.

Yvonne stumbled across it while running away from a half-dozen cops who were rounding up dirties. Hiding under the bridge, she'd spotted the latch and pried it open. She'd made a home out of the place, including pirated electricity, satellite television, and running water.

Yvonne holds the door open now as I help Kent into our concrete sanctuary. Kent's body is nearly completely melted and is draped over me like a soggy blanket. A heavy soggy blanket. "Hold on, Kent," I say. "Almost there."

"'Urrrry an' geat mee tae my rum," Kent says, having difficulty speaking because his jaw hangs down to his chest.

Kent's room contains a chair and desk, a couple of lamps, and an oak chest that he sleeps in. The furniture looks like it belongs in an old folk's home, not in a room belonging to an eighteen-year-old. Yvonne hurries inside and opens the chest. Struggling under the weight of Kent's formless body mass, I manage to hobble over to it. Yvonne and I pour Kent inside like a cake mix into a mold. She closes the lid, securing our friend snuggly inside.

I wipe the sweat from my brow and sigh. "He's lucky we're friends or I'd just let him ooze into the storm drain."

Lifelike plaster masks hang all over the walls in Kent's room. Each one is a mold of a person: skinny women, fat men, old folks, young kids. They give me the creeps. It's like all these people are inside the walls trying to escape. There's an unfinished mask resting on the desk. "Who's he working on now?" I ask.

"It's your birthday present," Yvonne says.

My birthday is next week, and I've told my friends that I won't accept gifts purchased with ill-gotten money. "What did I tell you about presents?"

"Hey, you only turn eighteen once."

I pick up the mask and see my face staring back at me. While still rough around the edges, it's clearly a mold of me. "I don't even want to know," I say. "But I'm taking this to make sure I don't land on the Most Wanted list."

Yvonne opens the lid to the chest, revealing Kent's gelatin-type translucent form, and bends down, placing her mouth close to the goo. "Kent, Marvin's taking his mask," she says.

There's a low gurgling sound and an air pocket forms near the bottom, then slowly rises to the top. It bubbles through the surface and pops, which produces a garbled "Laaammmeee."

If you're lucky, when your powers manifest you can still blend in with the normal people, or "normies" as we call them. But Kent isn't one of the lucky ones. He was born a normal-looking child, but with each passing year, his appearance slowly changed. All his bones and muscles are malleable, making his body flexible and pliant. He sleeps in the oak chest because he says he's most relaxed when he doesn't have to work to maintain a bodily form.

Kent's condition gives him some advantages, like being able to survive impacts that would kill someone else. I've actually witnessed him get hit by a car and walk away smiling, usually after extorting money from the driver to not file a police report. He can compress his body into small, tight places, making him a perfect thief. It didn't take him long to discover he could reshape his face to look like somebody else. To do this, he makes plaster masks to sculpt his gooey flesh. Kent has become incredibly talented at making molds based on photos, replicating facial features to perfection.

Mortified by his grotesque appearance, Kent's hillbilly parents kicked him out of their trailer when he was twelve. They didn't have the money to pay for him to go to the Power Aversion Program, and, even if they did, I don't know if the program could have made him normal. There's always talk about new breakthroughs in medicine to cure people who have dirty powers. The new fad is DNA-strand modification that will "repair" our molecular composition. Kent lived on the streets for three years before he crossed paths with Yvonne, and she, always the mothering type, welcomed him into her home with open arms.

"Are you scheduled to *work* tonight?" Yvonne asks me, looking up from the trunk. She rolls her eyes while she says this.

"What do you have against my job?"

"Nothing—if you were a normie. But you're one of us."

"But I obey the law."

Before disappearing to her room, she says, "Sometimes obeying the law isn't the right choice."

THREE

Surveying the mountain of dirty dishes, I slip on rubber gloves. I've lobbied the owner of the Midtown Café for a job as a waiter, because then I'd make real money from all the tips. But I'm stuck with bussing and dishwashing, since Gus says he never hires high school students as servers—school should be my top priority. That always ends the conversation. I'm certain he knows I'm a dropout, but it's a conversation we've never actually had. It's like Gus is toying with me, daring me to confide in him.

I turn on the hot water to fill up the sink, squirt in dish soap, and begin washing the dishes. My job isn't glamorous, and it tends to be tedious, but it's legal.

The Clean Powers Act was signed into law before I was born. The controversial bill established a department with the authority to certify powers as either "clean" or "dirty." When an individual's powers manifest, that person must register with the department and be subjected to a blood test. It doesn't take more than a minute to have the technician tie off your arm, find a vein, and take the blood. It's shipped off to a lab on the East Coast, and the results are mailed back within a week or two.

My test was a nightmare from the get-go. The nurse couldn't find a suitable vein no matter how tightly she cinched the rubber hose around my arm. She unapologetically stabbed me with a needle three times before she managed to extract enough blood to fill the test tubes. And to add insult to injury, when the results came back they were attached to a bright red stamp that read *DIRTY*. This meant that my powers were "unstable" and that I was a perceived danger to myself and others if I used them. It was explained to me that being dirty and using your powers is like driving an 18-wheeler with faulty brakes—you never know when you could lose control.

While my parents had always argued, having a son diagnosed as dirty was the beginning of the end. My father wanted me to go to the Power Aversion Program and hopefully take DNA-strand modification meds. "Marvin will be normal," he said. But my mother would have none of it. "Let him be who he is. He's perfect just the way he is."

They say the Power Aversion Program is voluntary, which I guess is true. But if a dirty doesn't enroll, it seems to attract a lot of attention from the government. My father had had run-ins with the law since before he was a teenager, and he certainly didn't want any unnecessary attention directed his way because of me.

For people whose blood tests are determined to be clean, fame and fortune are in the cards because they become authorized to use their powers for monetary compensation. Being dirty is the opposite—it's a label that makes you a pariah, prohibiting you from using your powers to earn a living.

And that's pretty much why I'm standing over this stainless steel sink washing dishes. I obey the law. Yvonne and Kent don't. I've lost count how many times I've told my friends it's just a matter of time until they get nabbed. They joke there isn't money in obeying the law and they'd rather get clipped than be poor.

"Marvin Maywood, you were late," a cheerful voice booms behind me. It's not hard to see that Gus was a handsome man thirty years ago, but years of playing hard and working hard have taken a toll. I'd guess he's in his early sixties. His brown skin is leathery and cracked, and his hands are calloused and scarred.

"How'd you know I was late?" I ask. "You weren't here when I came in."

Gus picks up a dishtowel and begins drying the dishes, stacking them to the side. "You're right, I wasn't here."

"Who ratted on me?"

"You just did," Gus smiles, nudging me with his shoulder. "You pay more attention in school, you might actually learn something."

My smile fades, which I'm sure doesn't escape my boss's attention. *Here we go again*, I think, *talking about school*.

"Did you hear about Streak?" he asks.

My heart skips a beat and my mouth is suddenly dry as the desert. "What about him?"

"Some dirties drugged him today in the park." Gus laughs. "Can you believe that? It's been on the news all day."

"Do they ... do they know who did it?"

"Some kids. But Lieutenant Mercury said that he won't rest until the Core uncovers who's responsible."

A plate slips out of my hand and drops to the floor, shattering into a cascade of porcelain. "Oh man, oh man, oh man!" I mumble.

Gus grabs a broom and a dustpan and sweeps up the broken plate. "It's okay, Marvin. Accidents happen."

Stunned, I watch as Gus cleans up my mess. His words, as ominous as a death sentence, ring in my ears. Lieutenant Mercury is going to attempt to find out who's responsible for drugging Streak.

Most people generally consider Lieutenant Mercury to be the first costumed hero. There were a few before, but none were introduced to the world like the masked man in yellow and black was. It was a public relations blitz, or so I'm told. He had his coming-out party before I was born, but I hear people all the time say that everyone knows where they were when they first heard about him.

He's the leader of the Core, so he's featured prominently in my collectibles. He sits at the head of the clean class, setting the bar high for everyone who's followed. Growing up, I wanted badly to be just like him. When my powers manifested, I thought it might actually become a reality, but reality came crashing down on me when I tested dirty. Mercury is as clean as you can get.

Gus dumps the pieces of porcelain into the garbage and looks at me, a concerned expression on his face. "What's gotten into you?" he asks. "Are you okay?"

I go back to washing dishes. I can feel him staring at me, but I refuse to look his way. I'm worried he'll see right through me and realize it was Yvonne, Kent, and me who had the unfortunate run-in with Streak.

14

He comes up beside me and begins to dry the dishes again. "Marvin, if you're ever in any kind of trouble," he says, "you know that you can come to me, right?"

"Trouble? I don't have any trouble," I say.

"You can run away all you want, but your wounds travel with you."

"Who said I was a runaway?"

"I said 'run away,' not 'runaway.'" Gus laughs.

"Well, I'm not—"

He raises his hands to silence me. "It's important to surround yourself with a strong support group," he says. "Friends and family that you can turn to for guidance. Do you have this sort of support group?"

"Yeah, of course," I say. "I have friends."

"Do you have friends or do you have friends?"

"Huh?"

"Are they friends who move you toward your goals?" he asks. "Are they friends who you can act like your normal self around? Friends should bring out the best in you, and if they don't, then you should find new ones. Put a rose in a sack of fish and soon the rose will start to stink, too."

Are Yvonne and Kent supportive of my goals? I think about them harassing me about my job and my decision not to use my powers to make money. I think about Yvonne telling me to stop trying to be something I'm not. Do my friends bring out the best in me? Do they move me closer to my goals? Well, if I'm being honest with myself, I suppose that I'd have to say—

Gus tosses the drying rag at me. "Now if you'll excuse me, I've got real work to do." He walks out of the kitchen.

I never have a conversation with Gus where I don't end up wondering whether he knows more about me than he's letting on. It's the way he says things, and how he asks questions, that makes me think he's asking something else entirely. It could be my imagination, but sometimes he looks strangely at me when I talk to him, as if he's disappointed by what I'm saying. I don't know what he wants from me. It's like he's waiting for me to do or say something, but I don't have a clue what that is. I wish he'd just tell me, because I'm not a mind reader.

FOUR

When I finish putting away the dishes and stocking the refrigerator, the restaurant is empty. All the cooks and waitresses are gone for the night. Even Gus skedaddled. Three weeks ago he gave me a key to the place, saying I'd earned his trust to close up at night. He taught me how to enter the code for the security system and arm it when I leave. When I told Yvonne and Kent about having a key, they'd begged me to go back and let them raid the refrigerator and beer cooler. I told them not a snowball's chance in hell. It means a lot that Gus has faith in me, and I'm not about to do anything that would destroy that trust.

Making the rounds through the restaurant, I turn off all the lights, unplug the neon signs, and make sure all the exits are locked. As I pass the counter, I spot a small stack of cash resting on top of two Styrofoam to-go containers with my name written on them. I pick up the cash and count it. After my first week on the job, Gus handed me a check. I'm sure my blank expression prompted my new boss to ask whether or not I had a bank account, and I admitted I didn't. He took the check and counted out the amount in cash. Ever since then, he always gives me cash, no questions asked.

Pocketing the money, I open the Styrofoam containers and am pleasantly surprised to find they contain leftover baby back ribs, one of Midtown Café's specialties. Gus usually squirrels away food for me that was just going to be tossed out at the end of the night. Yvonne and Kent love this job perk.

Juggling the to-go containers, I arm the security system, wait for the chirp, and hurry out the front door. On the street, the bus at the stop closes its doors. I sprint through the parking lot as it pulls away. "Wait!" I yell, waving my free hand. But the vehicle coughs a cloud of black exhaust as it ambles off. I stand on the sidewalk and watch as its tail lights fade into the city's artificial glare.

Tucking the containers under my arm, I hoof it down the street. It's not a long walk home—no more than five or six miles—certainly not long enough to kill me. But it's not the walk through a jungle that will kill you. It's the predators.

The street is deserted, not a car in sight. It reminds me of a post-apocalyptic landscape in the movies. It wouldn't surprise me a bit if tumbleweed rolled down the road, driven by a lonely wind. A street sweeper slowly drives by me on Elm Street. Thousands of bristles spin against the pavement, but it does little to remove the stains. Some stains just can't be brushed away.

As I turn down Red Hill Avenue, I spot a shiny SUV on the side of the street. There's a family of three—a father, mother, and a young boy, probably eight or nine years old—huddled around the back of the vehicle. The father pumps the jack up and down, up and down, slowly raising the backside of the SUV off the ground. The culprit is a flat tire. Despite this late-night inconvenience, the family laughs and appears to be in good spirits. The father nudges the young boy with his hip, which makes the boy howl with glee. The mother cups a hand over her mouth as she laughs.

I can't help but smile.

But almost immediately I'm gripped by a sense of loss, which is strange because I've never had this type of relationship with my father. Can you lose something that you've never had?

I'm nearly a block away from the family when I see four teenagers appear like specters out of the shadows. The smile on the father's face disappears as he sees the teens approach like jackals closing in on a wounded animal. He fumbles with the jack, frantically pumping it.

One of the hoodlums points and laughs. The young boy turns to look, but his mother whispers to him to not stare. He looks at his parents, confusion on his face as he senses their agitation. Fear swirls around them like a bad odor.

The teenagers surround the terrified trio. The ringleader has a pockmarked and twitchy face, like he has a tic, which conjures the image of a nervous rodent. His hands are stuffed deep inside his sweatshirt pocket. He leans forward and angles to get a look at the flat tire. "Car troubles, huh?" he asks, flashing a yellow smile.

The mother wraps a protective arm around her son. The father glances at the ringleader and fumbles with the jack. "Yeah...yes, a flat tire," he says.

"That sucks."

"We'll manage."

The ringleader whistles as he takes in the shiny SUV, then says, "This is a pimp ride you got."

"Thanks," the father says.

"This SUV ain't no joke. This must've set you back," the ringleader says.

The street sweeper turns onto Red Hill Ave and heads toward the SUV. The father jumps up and waves his arms. The city vehicle slows down and comes to a stop, and the driver leans out the window. "Car problems?" he asks.

The hoodlum nearest to the mother pulls a machete from under his jacket. He uses the blade to motion for the driver to move on. "Ain't nothin' to see here, old man."

"You snot-nosed little punk!" the driver barks.

Smiling, the ringleader pulls a small revolver out of his sweatshirt pocket and levels it at the driver. "You best be bouncin' outta here."

The city worker hesitates for only a moment before driving away. He disappears around the corner without so much as a backward glance.

The ringleader levels the gun at the father. "Now hand over your wallet and your lovely wife's purse," he hisses.

One of the hoodlums nudges the ringleader and motions toward me. "Check shorty."

All eyes turn to me, where I've been standing on the sidewalk watching the events unfold. "Hey, Slim, time for you to bounce," the ringleader shouts. "We's conducting business."

It would be so easy to walk away. Just keep walking and don't look back. I could forget this little incident ever happened.

I look at all the faces staring at me. The one that draws

my attention is the young boy. Tears run down his face, and his eyes are full of fear. He mouths the word *help*. It's a silent prayer, and, unfortunately for me, I'm the only one around to hear it.

I set the Styrofoam containers down on the ground and head toward the hoodlums. "What's your name, kid?" I ask.

The ringleader snarls, then snaps, "Ain't none of your business what my name is!"

"I was talking to the boy."

"Jack ... Jackson," the boy stammers. "Jackson James."

"Jackson, it's okay you're afraid ... because I'm afraid, too." My heart beats faster and my palms are sweaty.

The hoodlums don't know what to make of me as I stroll toward them. The scumbag with the machete jumps toward me, tossing the machete from hand to hand. A forced smile cracks across his face. "You don't want none of this," he says.

The ringleader taps the barrel of the revolver against the back of the father's head. "Slim, you's playing a dangerous game right now," he says. "You best be thinking twice 'bout what you's planning."

Holding Jackson's stare, I say, "I'm just going to need a little taste."

A puzzled look falls across the young boy's face. "Huh?" he croaks.

Closing my eyes, I tilt back my head as pressure builds at the center of my being, intensifying until it feels like it's going to overwhelm me. It's as if all my cells are in a choir and singing in perfect unison. I open my eyes with a start and say, "It's time to spread some of this fear around."

Having heard enough, the hoodlum clutching the machete brings the blade down at my head like a tomahawk. My hand shoots up and catches the sharp blade in my palm. The shocked teenager's eyes blink repeatedly, as if he can't believe that the blade didn't slice through my hand. In one seamless motion, I rip the machete out of his grasp and send it flying across the street. It punctures the side of the building, lodging there like Excalibur in the stone.

The hoodlum glances at the machete, then turns to me and says, "He's got powers."

Grabbing a handful of his shirt, I lift him off the ground and fling him. He flies through the air, screaming, until he slams against the building with a dull thud. His unconscious body drops to the ground.

I hear the explosion of the ringleader's revolver behind me. Moving faster than human eyes can detect, I spin around just in time to see the bullet hurtling toward my head. While I'm not indestructible, I can move super fast, which allows me to dodge a bullet like it's a fastball. The ringleader squeezes off four more rounds. I dodge the next three bullets but don't move fast enough to avoid the last one, which hits me in the shoulder. "Sonavabitch!" I yell, touching the bleeding wound with my hand. A plume of gunpowder hangs in the air.

The hoodlum grabs Jackson and points the barrel of the revolver flush against the side of his head. The young boy cries as the hot metal burns his skin. "Don't freakin' move!" the ringleader yells.

Having seen enough, the two unarmed hoodlums trip over themselves as they stumble away, fleeing into the night.

The ringleader keeps the gun against the boy's head as he

backs away. "This is how it's gonna work," he shouts. "I'm gettin' outta here with the boy. Got it?!"

"You're not leaving with the boy," I say, trying to remember how many bullets were shot. One. Two. Three. Four. Five. Only five. There's one more bullet.

"Oh yes I am!" the gun-wielding thug hollers. "You better believe that!"

Jackson's parents watch helplessly as their son is ripped away from them. "Please don't," the father says. "I'll give you whatever you want, just let my son go."

"Don't take my baby," the mother sobs.

The ringleader shouts, "Shut up! Shut up. I'm leaving or the boy sucks on a bullet. Got it?!" He pulls Jackson close as he backs into an alley.

In a blur, I speed toward them. I reach out and grab hold of Jackson, pulling him out of the thug's grasp. Clutching the boy to my chest, I run him to safety behind the SUV. The ringleader hasn't even had time to process that he no longer has a grip on the young boy as I connect my clenched fist to the side of his head. He flies through the air twenty feet and then slams into a lamppost. I hear bones breaking as he drops to the ground, the revolver clanking out of his hand into the gutter.

The hoodlum's shallow breath is raspy. I exhale a sigh of relief that I didn't kill him. He might walk with a limp, but he'll live.

The parents run to their son. The family embraces, hugging and kissing each other, relieved they all survived the ordeal.

Checking my gunshot wound, I know I'm lucky. It just grazed me.

"Thank you, mister," Jackson says. The whole family holds one another and smiles at me. "What's your name?"

Without thinking, I say, "Marvin."

"What kinda hero name is that?"

"Who said I'm a hero?"

The boy looks confused. "But ... that's what you are."

Jackson doesn't know me. He doesn't know that I'm dirty, or that my powers are fed by fear. That's not heroic and certainly not clean. But as I stare at the starry-eyed boy, I don't have the energy or the desire to explain this to him. I speed off in a blur to get home before I black out.

FIVE

I know I'm asleep. It's one of those dreams where you know you're dreaming and you're trying to wake up but you can't. I'm paralyzed, rooted in place, unable to shake away my slumber. I become aware of something big approaching in the distance. I feel it in the ground beneath me. The roar builds with the vibration that rattles my teeth. My whole body shakes as the ground hums.

This is when I start to panic.

I try to open my eyes, but my lids open just a crack, enough to see blinding light. My vision is blurry and distorted and the brightness desperately hurts my eyes, like I'm staring up at the sun. A giant wave of air whooshes over me. Tiny particles of dust and debris pelt my face. In my dream, I scream like a banshee, thrashing my head around, hoping my body gets the wake-up call.

I sit up with a start right as an 18-wheeler barrels past me. I'm sitting in a ditch on the side of the freeway. My mouth is dusty and dry, and I try to spit but it's a desert. Dirt and grime crunch between my teeth. I remember racing toward home and nothing else. I'd tried to get back home before I crashed, but obviously that didn't work out.

Groaning, I slowly get to my feet. I dust myself off, then cover my eyes with a hand and look around. In the distance, I see the Edinger Avenue overpass. I nearly made it. As I walk along the shoulder, I wonder how many people saw me lying there. I would've been in plain sight. I don't know whether or not I'm grateful that nobody stopped to investigate. I pat my front pocket and feel the wad of cash from Gus. Nobody rolled me while I was out, so at least that's something.

I look toward the sky and figure it's early afternoon. I was probably out for twelve hours or so, but this is normal. After I use my powers, I crash like a drug addict after a binge.

A stabbing pain in my stomach causes me to double over. It feels like my stomach is turning in on itself. I wait until the pain passes and hurry toward home. I curse under my breath that I forgot the Styrofoam boxes of leftovers. That food would hit the spot right about now. I'm ravenous. Whenever I wake up after using my power, I eat like a herd of starving elephants. I once added up the calories during one of these binges, and it was more than a normal person eats in a week. I need to eat, and I need to eat now.

The continuous hum of vehicles vibrates through the overpass as I make my way down the corridor to the kitchen. I open the refrigerator and grumble that it's empty. There's a cereal box on the counter. I pick it up and dump the Corn Flakes into my mouth. I chew loudly and swallow. Dry cereal never tasted so good. But this half-empty box of cereal won't be enough. Not by a long shot.

I push past the raggedy blanket I use as a door for my room. Yvonne is curled up on my bed, asleep. The bedside lamp casts her in a warm light. Her jeans and sweatshirt are two sizes too big. Her hair is held back in a ponytail, secured by a rubber band. But despite this, she's cute. I get a twinge of something that resembles longing, but quickly shake away the notion as being completely inappropriate, like thinking a cousin is attractive. Gross.

I dump the rest of the cereal into my mouth and chew loudly, which causes Yvonne to stir. As I retrieve a clean shirt, she sits up. "Marvin, what the hell?!" She jumps off the bed. "Are you okay?"

"Yeah," I say, removing my shirt and putting on a clean one.

"We were really worried about you. What happened last night?" Her eyes look like they belong to an adult. She's seen way too much for someone her age.

"I've got to eat something. I'm dying. Wanna go? My treat."

"But what—"

I step out into the corridor. "Let's get Kent."

Kent's sitting at the desk in his room, using a tiny chisel to clear away slight imperfections in the plaster of a new mask. He lifts up his sagging face and says, "It's been a long day and I don't think I can hold it together much longer."

"Do you want anything?" I ask.

"You can tell me why you had to use your powers last night," he says.

"Oh, it was nothing," I say. My friends share a knowing smile. "What?"

Yvonne pretends to hold a microphone and speaks into it. "Son, can you tell us what happened?" she asks.

Kent lifts his hands to his face and, in a childlike voice, says, "He single-handedly saved me and my mom and dad from four bad men. He moved faster than Streak and was as strong as Lieutenant Mercury. He was amazing."

"And who is this hero?"

"He said his name was Marvin."

"Marvin?"

"Yeah, Marvin."

"If you could say one thing to Marvin," Yvonne asks, "what would it be?"

"Marvin, you're my hero," Kent squeals. Satisfied with their taunting, my friends turn to me, waiting for an explanation.

"Oh, crap, it was on the news?" I say.

"Yep." Yvonne smiles. "Every channel this morning."

"What were you thinking?" Kent asks. "Did you think you were clean?"

"I wasn't about to let those thugs jump that family," I say.

"But why'd you tell them your name? Now everybody knows about this mysterious Marvin kid who saves motorists." Yvonne groans.

Dismissing her with a wave of my hand, I say, "Nobody knows who I am." Kent shoots Yvonne a look.

She glares at him. "Just say it."

"Lieutenant Mercury does," Kent shoots back.

Kent and I never say the name Lieutenant Mercury in front of Yvonne. I don't know what the deal is, but it's like fingernails on a chalkboard to her. She really doesn't like the guy, and she's never explained why.

"Hold it...what?" I say. "Lieutenant Mercury knows about it?"

Yvonne grimaces at the mention of his name. "Yeah. They had a sound bite from him on the news."

"What did he say?"

"While he 'admires anyone who comes to the aide of others,' he 'hopes the person isn't dirty,'" Kent tells me.

"And he wants you to pay a visit to the Core Mansion so you two can discuss the matter," Yvonne adds.

"He said that?"

"I know, right?" Kent laughs. "What a tool."

"Like you're stupid enough to roll up to the Core Mansion," Yvonne says. "They'd neuter you."

"But it would be nice to check the place out," Kent mutters.

I nod my head, agreeing with him.

"It's that kind of thinking that will get us nabbed," Yvonne snaps.

She and I find a quiet booth at Eat-A-Rama, an all-you-can-eat buffet, which is just what the doctor ordered to satisfy my hellacious appetite. I clear two plates before Yvonne joins me with her tray, which consists of salad.

"So, the Core, huh? You'd like to be a member?"

"Who wouldn't?" I say.

"Did you know that more members of the Core kill themselves than die in the line of duty?" she asks.

I set my fork down and swallow my food, wiping my mouth with the napkin. "Oh, come on."

"It's true," she says. "What does that tell you about their outfit? They have secrets and agendas we don't know about."

"I don't even know what you're talking about."

"Marvin, if you put your faith in institutions like the Core, they're going to let you down every single time. How many dirties and cleans are there? Two, three million maybe? Most are dirty, like us, trying to blend in or enrolling in the Power Aversion Program."

While I was still living at home, I'd desperately tried to blend in and go unnoticed, but that was easier said than done. When my father drank, it was hard to escape his attention, and whenever it became clear that he was coming after me in a drunken rage, my mother would try to distract him and protect me. While I was trying to go unnoticed and blend in, she was sacrificing herself for her child. I could've—should've—acted, but I didn't.

I won't do that again. Ever.

I pick at my food with my fork. "It felt good."

"What did?"

"Helping that family," I say.

"Yeah?"

"For that brief time, I forgot about me, my life, and just was."

"Was what?"

"Was someone better."

She slides her plate across the table and sets her napkin down. "That sounds like something my father would say." A sad smile brushes across her face.

This is the first time Yvonne has ever spoken to me about her parents. Kent told me that she once showed him a childhood picture of when she was two or three, with her mom and dad at the shore of a lake. But that's the extent of her discussing her past, particularly anything about her parents. This is fine with me because I don't talk about my parents either.

As we walk home, she asks, "Do you ever think about having DNA-strand modification?"

"Having my powers removed?" I say.

"Yeah."

"I made a promise that I wouldn't."

"To who?"

"My mom. Right before she died."

Yvonne opens her mouth to say something, but then changes her mind. I'm glad, because I don't want to talk about it anymore.

"Isn't it ironic?" she says. "We have powers, but we're powerless."

SIX

After drying and putting all the dishes away, I take out the garbage, put the crates of food into the walk-in refrigerator, and sweep and mop the floor.

The two cooks sit on barstools and play a game of cards.

I head out to the dining area and find the waitress sitting at the counter working a crossword puzzle. Gus sits next to her with his nose buried in a newspaper. There are a couple of customers scattered through the restaurant, but it's definitely not a busy night. I grab a wet towel and go about wiping down the tables.

"Did you hear about that family, saved a few blocks from here?" Gus asks, looking at me.

I nod my head yes, not trusting my voice.

"Do you know anything about it?"

I shake my head no.

Gus studies me for a moment, then turns his attention back to the newspaper. "The cops came by here this morning and asked if I saw anything last night." He digs into his shirt pocket and pulls out a business card. "One of them gave me his card and told me to call if I thought of anything."

The waitress scribbles on the puzzle and says, "The guy who saved the family said his name was Marvin."

"It wasn't you, was it?" Gus asks, looking at me.

"I wish," I say, my smile forced and wide.

The waitress nudges Gus in the ribs with her elbow. "Why would someone with powers work here?"

Gus's eyes linger on me for a moment. I can't help but feel he's trying to read me like the newspaper open in front of him.

I wonder what Gus would do if I told him it *was* me who saved the family. If I had to tell a normie, I'd probably choose him. There have been several occasions when I nearly told him the truth, but then I never do because of something I overheard him say once. I'd only been working at Midtown Café a couple of weeks. Gus was standing behind the counter, refilling the coffee cups of the crusty old-timers. A man with a nose ravaged by gin blossoms poured a stream of sugar into his coffee. "Clean or dirty, got no stomach for their kind. Bunch a freaks, all of 'em."

I was used to this type of sentiment. I did my best to ignore it and not take it too personally. It wasn't hard to dismiss bigotry from strangers. The difficulty arose when it was someone you knew and liked.

Then Gus said, "You know the difference between the members of the Core and God? God doesn't think he's a member of the Core."

The old-timers slapped the countertop as they roared with laughter. Gus's smile faded when he spotted me staring at him.

It's that one lingering memory that makes me keep him at arm's length.

Gus tells the waitress she can leave for the night, and she hurries off, evidently on her way to something more fun. As she leaves, a woman passes her in the doorway. She's dressed like she's stepped out of a fashion magazine. "Are you still open?" she asks.

"Sit anywhere," I say. She sits down at a booth and I approach her with a menu. "We're going to be closing soon, so you might want to decide quickly."

Getting a closer look, I realize that she's young—probably my age, maybe a little younger. She's attractive. Her long blond hair looks like every strand is meticulously placed. She has thick, full lips and olive skin that radiates a healthy glow. She looks familiar, but I can't place her. I find myself staring at her, and it takes me a moment to realize she's staring back at me with her big brown eyes. While her expression doesn't betray any emotion, her eyes seem to smile. I get a whiff of the heady aroma of a bed of roses after a summer rain shower.

"I'm not going to order anything," she says. "But could I trouble you for a glass of water?"

I gather up the menu and say, "You got it."

As I fill a glass with water, I steal peeks at the girl. I know I've seen her before. Maybe she's an actress or something. I wish I could place her. All I know is that she's stunning. It makes we wonder what on earth she's doing in a restaurant located in this part of town after sundown. I set the glass of water down on the table.

"What's your name?" she asks.

"Marvin."

"Of course it is. Silly me," she says. "I'm Eliza. Eliza Todd. I'm hoping we can have a little chat, Marvin."

"Really? What about?"

"About last night," Eliza says.

"Last night?"

"When you saved that family."

Time slows way down. I can feel my heart beating like a bass drum in my chest. The noise echoes in my ears. Her words smack me and take my breath away. I don't know how long I stand there and stare at her. My mind scrambles to make sense of what just happened. How does she know this?

My brain is like a blank sheet of paper, and the glaring emptiness is too harsh a sight to maintain, so I turn and hurry away, disappearing through the kitchen door. I rest my back against the wall, trying to calm myself. It feels like I'm going to hyperventilate.

Peeking through the window in the door, I see her across the restaurant, smiling at me. I duck out of sight.

When I finally muster up the courage to steal another peek, I see Gus locking up for the night. There's no sign of the girl.

———

Before Gus leaves, he asks if I'll tidy up his office. I don't mind because I need the money. The job takes longer than I expected, though, because Gus is a slob. There are empty candy wrappers, soda cans, and garbage strewn about like it's a landfill. While I'm on the floor crawling around on my hands and knees, I see that Gus has made a habit of parking his used gum under his desk. There's so much of it that it looks like a mural under there. Retrieving a butter knife, I chisel away at the dried gum.

Finally finished, I stroll out of the office and head back to the kitchen to wash the butter knife before I lock up. As I round the corner, heading back behind the counter, I hear someone speak.

"Hey," the soft voice says. Eliza sits in the same booth as before. It's like she's been there the whole time.

"What're you doing?" I ask.

"Our conversation was cut short," she says. "We need to discuss last night."

"You're not supposed to be here," I say.

She motions to my hand. "Are you going to stab me?"

I'm still holding the butter knife, and I clutch it like I'm planning on using it against her. "How'd you get in?" I ask.

"I hid in the women's bathroom."

"You've got to go."

She motions to the seat across from her. "Let's talk, then I'll leave."

I stand there a moment and weigh my options. I can grab her and force her out, call the cops, or listen to what she has to say. But I don't like the idea of getting rough with her. And if I call the cops, she might blab about me saving the family. Even if she can't prove it, I don't need any unnecessary attention. I slide into the booth across from her. "Two minutes," I say. "That's it."

She reaches across the table and takes my hands in hers. "The Core has decided to let you try out for the team."

I rip my hands out of hers as if she's contagious, and,

who knows, maybe she is. "Who are you?!" I say, my voice going up two octaves.

She leans back in her seat and says, "I'm Roisin."

A revelation of this magnitude would normally be earth-shattering. But the way she flippantly offers this tidbit of information—as if she were commenting on something inconsequential like the weather—leaves me feeling like I just received the "answer" but didn't know the question. She's just claimed to be Roisin, the youngest hero to ever join the Core.

After a moment of me just staring at her, she laughs and asks, "You heard me, right?"

"Yeah."

"And?"

I don't say anything.

"You're strange. I like strange. And it helps you're kinda cute too," she says.

I tend to trust people until they give me reason not to, but this, I don't know. It's a whole lot to take on face value. "Prove it," I say.

"How?"

"Change into your costume."

"I didn't bring it."

"Why not?"

"Wasn't planning on wearing it tonight."

"Um, okay," I mumble. "So, why all white?"

"Excuse me?"

"Why an all-white costume?"

She extends a hand and inspects her fingernails, which are painted with a sparkly silver polish. Tilting her head to the side, she says, "I like that people see me coming."

"Do that light-from-the-eyes thingy."

"In here? That's not a good idea. This place'll get torched. It's hot enough to burn concrete."

"Okay, then walk on air. You do that, right?"

She shakes her head and says, "I can walk on anything that's denser than air, like water or something like that."

"Then how're you gonna prove you're Roisin? Isn't that all you can do?"

Leaning across the table, she whispers, "Can you keep a secret?" I nod my head. "I can boil water with the touch of my finger."

"You can?"

"As sure as I'm sitting here."

"I've never heard that about Roisin," I say.

"It's a secret."

"Why?"

"Our PR people worried that it was too insignificant."

"PR people?"

"Public relations," she says. "Go get me a cup of water."

I slide out of the booth, go behind the counter, and grab a coffee cup, which I fill with tap water. I spill a little as I walk back to the table. "Is this enough?"

"This'll do," she says, sticking her finger into the water and twirling it around like she's mixing creamer into coffee. "Ta-da!"

Steam rises from the cup. I stick my finger in the liquid and it burns. "Yep. It's hot."

"Do you believe me now?" she asks.

"You've got powers. That's for sure."

"So how about it? You wanna try out for the Core?"

SEVEN

As we stand outside Midtown Café, Eliza says, "You can't tell anyone about this."

"Why?"

"The members of the Core live under constant scrutiny. We can't go out for ice cream without everyone talking about it. We need to know that you can be trusted to keep this quiet," she says. "If it leaks, we'll know it was you, so don't risk it by telling anyone. Not a peep."

She gets into her shiny orange sports car and rides the gas hard. Her speedster spins out as she maneuvers out of the parking lot. I wonder if she's actually old enough to drive. But I figure being a member of the Core has its benefits.

A yellow cab rumbles past, and I wave my hand and whistle. The car crosses two lanes and pulls up to me. I open the door and climb in back. "Where to?" the cabbie asks.

I tell him, and he raises an eyebrow. Pulling out the wad of cash Gus left me tonight, I hold it up to show him I have money. He flips on the meter and merges into traffic. I don't blame the guy for being leery of heading into the belly of the beast—the old downtown. Gangs, pimps, and your garden-variety lowlifes overrun this area like weeds. I'd clean it up if I were a member of the Core. (Just thinking this sends a shiver through my body. It's just too perfect a thought for me to consider.)

We ride through the Loganstin business district. Buildings that reach for the sky house the titans of industry. These movers and shakers trade in commodities I can't even pronounce, much less understand. This part of town is all that's left to remind us of what Loganstin used to be. This is where the businessmen, lawyers, and politicians hold court. The streets are clean, the glass on the buildings shimmers under the sun, and hope springs eternal.

People like me aren't welcome in this part of town—at least not during the day. A few years back, two degenerate terrorists, Monger and Gunner, locked horns here. The dirties leveled the place. After that, the city tried to pass an ordinance banning the use of powers in the business district, but the Core was vocal in its opposition. The measure died, but the sentiment remains, along with an empty lot where the Grinde Investment Building used to stand. The structure had to be demolished after the battle due to extensive damage. The area is an ugly reminder of the destructive force of dirties.

The taxi takes a turn and it's like we enter another country. It's amazing how quickly the landscape can change in this city. The buildings are abandoned, run down, and covered in graffiti. Prostitutes mill about on street corners. Drug dealers hide in the shadows, ready to disappear if something bad goes down. The police stay away as much as possible. It has its own laws, and they're well outside of what the men and women in blue are supposed to enforce.

The taxi pulls to a stop in front of Broadway Liquor. "That'll be twenty bucks," the cabbie says. I peel off a couple of bills and hand them to him. Before I even have time to shut the door, the cabbie jams his car into gear and races down the street.

I find Yvonne in the alley next to the liquor store. Three junkies mill around her, offering her various things in exchange for a fix. One pulls out a ten-dollar bill and hands it over. She quickly pockets the money. The man wipes his runny nose with his sleeve. He twitches with anticipation as he waits for her to work her magic. Yvonne lays a hand on his shoulder, like she's greeting an old friend. Her eyes roll into the back of her head as she conjures her power. The effects of getting zapped make the junkie look like a marionette getting its strings cut. His legs wobble as he sways back and forth. It's as if he's moving to music only he can hear. He turns around and slowly slinks out of the alley toward me.

He's walking in a daze, and I don't even think he sees me as he staggers around the corner. He steps into the street, apparently unconcerned when a car blares its horn and swerves to avoid hitting him. Once he reaches the other side of the street, the junkie disappears into the dark crowd.

Another addict plops down on the cold concrete and slides off his dirty sneakers. Kneeling on the ground, he offers up the shoes. Yvonne turns her head away in disgust at the horrible stench coming out of them and says, "What am I gonna do with your crummy shoes? Come back when you have ten bucks." The guy doesn't even bother putting on his shoes as he sulks past me, mumbling under his breath about how unfair life is.

Yvonne's last customer pulls out a handful of crumpled bills and coins, holding them up like a child in a candy store asking how much he can buy with his allowance. Yvonne begrudgingly uses her finger to dig through the coins, seeing if he has enough. Apparently he does, because she takes the money and stuffs it into her pocket. She lays her hand on the junkie's head. Just before she closes her eyes, a small girl clutching a teddy bear steps out of the shadows and into the alley.

"Daddy, I'm hungry," the little girl says.

Startled, Yvonne opens her eyes, her hand recoiling from the man.

"Not now!" the man hisses. "Daddy's gettin' his medicine."

Yvonne is rattled. She can't take her eyes off the girl's filthy face and ragged dress. The stuffing of the bear is coming out of holes in its seams.

"Come on, Yvonne," the junkie pleads. "Do it."

"Is that your daughter?" Yvonne asks.

"Yeah."

Yvonne must see what I do—the junkie has no love for the girl. The only love this man has in his heart is for getting high. There just isn't enough room left over for his daughter.

I saw this same expression on my father's face when he used to look at me.

"What's her name?" Yvonne asks.

"Harriet," the junkie spits. "Now gimme my fix."

Yvonne takes a couple of steps toward the girl and says, "Hi, Harriet. My name is Yvonne."

"Everyone calls me Harry," the girl says.

"Okay. Hi, Harry."

"Gimme my fix!" the junkie yells. "Leave my daughter alone!"

Yvonne ignores the man. She kneels down next to the girl. "That sure is a nice teddy bear," she says. "What's its name?"

Harry looks from Yvonne to her father and back again. "Mr. Bear," she says, in not much more than a whisper.

"Nice name." Yvonne licks her thumb and tries to wipe away the grime from the girl's face. "Are you hungry, Harry?"

The little girl nods her head yes.

This scene is just too much for the junkie, and he rushes over and grabs his daughter by the arm, lifting her up and away from Yvonne. "I said to leave my daughter alone," he snaps. "I paid for my fix, so give it to me!"

I run into the alley, stopping Yvonne before she lunges at the man. "Yvonne, no!"

"I want my fix, bitch!" the junkie screams, gripping Harry by the arm.

Yvonne takes a couple of deep breaths, calming herself. "Okay, I'll give it to you," she says, "but only if you give me your daughter."

"What?!" both the junkie and I say at the same time.

"That's the deal," Yvonne says. "Take it or leave it."

The junkie lets go of Harry. "You want my daughter?"

"Because obviously you don't," Yvonne snaps.

The little girl begins to cry. "Daddy, don't," she sobs.

The junkie actually considers it.

"Yvonne, don't do this," I say.

"Why not?" Yvonne asks. "He doesn't deserve her."

Harry grabs her father's hand, pulling him away from Yvonne and me. "Let's go, Daddy. Please, let's go."

"Gimme my money back," the man says. "I'll score some dope off Filthy Mike."

Yvonne pulls his money from her pocket. The junkie reaches for it, but Yvonne drops the bills and coins on the ground. The coins clank on the concrete and scatter like ice from a spoon.

"You stupid bitch," he says, letting go of Harry's hand to retrieve his money.

Yvonne takes a ten-dollar bill out of her pocket and steps over to the little girl. As the junkie scurries on his dirty hands and knees, trying to gather his coins, she stuffs the bill into a rip in the teddy bear. "Don't tell your father about the money," she whispers. "Use it to get something to eat."

Harry looks at where the money is lodged inside Mr. Bear, then smiles at Yvonne. Before anything else can be uttered, the junkie storms over and grabs his daughter, pulling her out of the alley behind him.

Yvonne and I watch as the father and daughter walk away. She quickly wipes a tear from her eye, doing her best to conceal it from me.

"Tough day at the office?" I say.

She laughs, even though I realize she doesn't think it's particularly funny. And neither do I.

We get home and find Kent stretched out on the sofa with his eyes glued to a celebrity magazine. Yvonne sinks down next to him. Holding up the magazine for her to see, Kent says, "Dude, Roisin's claimin' she's a virgin."

Yvonne rips the magazine out of Kent's hands. "Shut up," she says.

Kent kneads his flesh like a baker shaping dough. "It's right there. Check it."

Yvonne says, "There's no way that tramp is a virgin."

"God, I hope not," Kent says. "That'll ruin all my fantasies about her."

"Oh my," Yvonne says, laughing. "Get a load of this photo." She turns the magazine around. The six members of the Core pose outside their mansion.

I focus on Roisin. After meeting her tonight, I can totally see it's the same person. If she was concerned about protecting her identity, you'd think she'd wear a more concealing mask.

Yvonne holds up a page that has a photo of Rocket. "I wonder if Rocket is ever bummed that he's the only non-white on the team?"

"Why the hell would he care?" Kent asks.

"I don't know," Yvonne says. "It would probably be nice to have someone else of color in your workplace."

"Nobody cares anymore what you look like," Kent says. "It's what's on the inside that matters: whether or not you have powers. That's the only currency that counts in this world. The color of your skin is as meaningless as your favorite number. Hell, it doesn't even matter if you're dumb as a sack of rocks. Which they have on the team."

"Since we're talking about the Core, you've got to narrow down the stupid list," Yvonne says.

"Your favorite. The leader."

"Oh, come on," I say. "Show some respect."

"I heard Mercury actually salutes his refrigerator because it's General Electric," Kent says.

"Oh yeah, well, I heard that when he was at a party at the White House, he flew up to the roof because he heard drinks were on the house." Yvonne snorts.

Kent is laughing so hard he's wiping tears from his drooping eyes. "He went to the lumber yard to meet the Board of Education," he says.

Yvonne and Kent are having a hard time catching their breath. "After Mystic walked by him on the sidewalk, he put his chin on the curb to get his mind outta the gutter," she says.

"And I heard he ate pennies and then asked the Core if they'd seen any change in him," Kent says.

When they get into a riff, Yvonne and Kent can go for hours. Dueling jokesters. Shaking my head, I get up and walk out of the living room.

Yvonne says, "He's so dumb he flew into a gun fight and got stabbed."

Heading into the darkness on the way to my room, I hear the echo of my friends' laughter behind me. I've endured their taunts before about my collection of Core memorabilia, and I good-naturedly laugh it off. Haters are going to hate. But now their joking about the Core really irritates me. It feels personal.

EIGHT

The taxi circles around the parking lot. Waving at the driver, I pile into the back seat of the vehicle. I give the driver the address, and he puts the car in gear and heads toward the freeway.

I double-check the address Eliza scribbled down on a piece of paper. At the restaurant the other night, she told me that if I wanted to engage in further discussion about trying out for the Core, I should meet her at this address.

"When?" I asked.

"Whenever," she replied.

"How about tomorrow morning?" I said. "I always work the night shift."

"I don't get out of bed until noon."

"I don't have a shift this weekend…"

"Sunday, then," she said. "But it'll have to be around five in the afternoon. I get outta bed late on the weekends too."

When she handed me the paper with the address, I said, "Really? Bixby Gardens?"

She assured me it was the place.

The taxi now travels down deserted surface streets lined with abandoned buildings. This is Bixby Gardens, Loganstin's main industrial zone. This area has been devastated over the years. The automotive jobs were outsourced to other countries, leaving behind sprawling factories that are shadowy and silent. Once glorious, these factories are now ravaged by rust and disintegrating mortar, reducing them to skeletal remains.

Forced to slow down because of a fallen tree in the middle of the road, the taxi driver rolls to a stop and turns off the meter, which reads thirty-five dollars and change. "This is as far as I can go," he says, pointing through the windshield. "The building you want should be just down there."

I hand over two twenties. "Keep the change," I say, sliding out of the taxi. The driver circles around and heads back the way he came.

The windows on the dilapidated three-story building have long been shattered. It appears that at some point, plywood was mounted to the front of the building to cover up the windows, but somebody kicked them in and now they lie on the ground covered in graffiti. Sticking my head into an open window frame, I get a raunchy whiff of something that's been decomposing for a while.

Double-checking the piece of paper, I say, "This is the place?"

Shattered glass crunches underfoot as I step into the building. A layer of ash covers everything. I run my finger along the wall and inspect the black smudge on my fingertip.

Heading deeper into the building, I find a rickety staircase. The structure moans under my weight as I head upstairs, wavering slightly with each step as I make my way to the second floor. All the rooms are empty. "She gave me the wrong address," I grumble.

Heading up another flight, I check the final floor and find more of the same—the exception being one room with the door shut, located at the end of the hall. The wood floor creaks underfoot. A warm light shines through a crack at the bottom of the door. Placing my ear against the door, I listen for any sound coming from the other side. I don't hear anything. Testing the knob, I find that it's unlocked.

The apartment is strangely clean and homey. The dark hardwood floors are polished and clean, the furniture looks brand new, and music plays softly through a sound system wired to every room. Daylight shines through the two windows in the living room. Paintings and framed photos of Loganstin landmarks are meticulously placed on the walls. Track lighting is positioned to shine on the art, basking it in a soft light. Somebody spent a lot of time getting this place into shape. They might be squatting in an abandoned building, but that obviously doesn't mean they have to live in squalor, as evidenced by the flat-screen television mounted on the wall.

"You made it," a voice says behind me.

Startled, I find Eliza—who's wearing a short silk bathrobe and has a towel wrapped around wet hair—sipping coffee from a mug. She leans against the wall and smiles at me.

"Oh, hey," I say. "I didn't know if this was your place or not. Sorry."

"Sorry? For what?"

"For barging in like this."

"Marvin, people like us don't have to say sorry," she says.

"This place is nice. Do you live here?"

"No, I live at the Core Mansion," she says.

"Oh, yeah, that makes sense," I mutter, feeling the fool. "All the members of the Core live at the mansion."

"This place is my own personal getaway. Like a safe house," she says. She finishes the last of her coffee and motions for me to follow her. "Let me give you a tour."

The stainless steel appliances and marble countertops in the kitchen look like a display in a home-improvement store. Eliza opens the dishwasher and sets her coffee mug inside, then removes a bottle of water from the refrigerator. "Do you want something to drink?" she asks.

"No, I'm okay."

She unscrews the cap on the bottle and lifts it to her lips, drinking deeply. She holds my gaze the entire time. A mischievous glimmer twinkles in her eyes. She breezes past me, so close her silk robe brushes against me. "Come."

We walk down the hall, and she enters a room that's a shrine to Roisin. There are posters hanging on the walls, many of which I've seen before in magazines, but some that I haven't. Glass cases are filled with Roisin dolls dressed entirely in white, including a complete collection of bobble heads that jiggle lightly, as if swaying in a phantom breeze.

"What do you think?" she asks.

"Wow."

"I know, right?"

"You collect Roisin…your memorabilia?"

"Yeah, I get a kick out of it," she says.

"Hey, what should I call you?" I ask. "Eliza or Roisin?"

"Roisin means 'Little Rose,'" she says. "It's a stage name, like something a stripper would use."

"Um ... okay."

"If I'm in costume, call me Roisin," she says. "But when we're alone, you can call me Eliza. And if everything goes as planned, we'll be spending a lot of time alone." She gives me a wink.

Blood rushes to my cheeks. Embarrassed, I inspect the nearest glass case. There's a Roisin action figure holding hands with a male figurine wearing a skintight black outfit, chiseled muscles outlined underneath, and a blue mask that only covers his eyes. "Who's that?" I ask.

Eliza comes up behind me and rests her chin on my shoulder, gazing at the action figures. "Oh, that's Blackbird."

"I've never heard of him."

"He was a recruit from a small crew on the East Coast. He tried out for a spot on the Core. We were supposed to hook up or something," she says. "At least, that's what was going to be marketed."

"Really?"

"Yeah, they were in the process of making these action figures of us as a couple. I didn't really mind. He was hot, that's for sure. He was killed in a freak training accident."

"Oh, man, I'm sorry."

She shrugs and says, "You get into this game, you're going to know people who die." She gives my hand a squeeze. "Don't worry. You'll be fine if you listen to me and do everything that I tell you to do."

The sound of a machine whirring comes from behind a closet door that's slightly ajar. "What's in there?" I ask.

Eliza closes the door. There's a security keypad mounted over the doorknob, and she presses the 6 key three times, which triggers the sound of a heavy lock sliding into place. She glances back at me but I look away, not wanting her to catch me watching her key in the passcode. A tiny green light on the keypad turns red. Eliza flashes me a warm smile and says, "I keep my computer in there."

"Keep it behind lock and key, huh?" I chuckle.

"Do you know how many people would love to see what's on the computer of a member of the Core? Hell, even at the Core Mansion, Security monitors what songs I download. I've got to be careful. That's why I have this place. It's completely off the grid." She grabs my hand and pulls me along behind her, leading me into a room at the end of the hall. "Come see my bedroom."

The bedroom has a four-poster bed, a chest of drawers, and a television mounted on the wall. Curtains are drawn over the windows.

"Nice room," I say.

"You should see my room at the Core Mansion," she says. "But this one isn't so bad."

She opens a drawer and removes underwear and a bra. Before I realize what's happening, she's untying the belt around her waist and beginning to remove the bathrobe. I spin around with my back to her. "Sorry," I mutter, my eyes gazing down at my feet.

She giggles. "Such a gentleman. You're sweet." A moment passes, and then she says, "Okay, it's safe to look." She's wearing her underwear and bra. She removes the towel from around her head, and her hair falls to her shoulders. She tilts her head to the side and pats her damp hair with the towel.

If my emotions were measured like a speedometer, I'd be clocked doing 125 mph. I have never been around someone who makes me as uncomfortable as Eliza—but uncomfortable in an exciting way.

"So, when's the last time you talked to your father?"

"My father?" I ask, hoping I heard her wrong.

"Yeah."

"What do you know about him?"

"I know that he killed your mother during a domestic dispute," she says. "He's serving a ten-year stint in prison."

My stomach ties into a knot, and it feels like my tongue suddenly swells and gets stuck in the back of my throat. "How do you know all this?" I ask, laboring over each word.

She tosses the towel onto the bed and shakes her hair. "Marvin, Marvin, Marvin," she says. "This is a courtship, and I won't give it up until I know you're a good fit."

I wasn't prepared for this slap of reality. I've never told Yvonne or Kent about my father. I've tried desperately to bury the memories deep inside me. If I could wipe it from my mind I'd do it in a heartbeat, even if it means erasing all the fond memories of my mother, who died to protect me. The pain is too raw. And Eliza just opened the can of worms like it's the most inconsequential topic ever—like asking me who was my first kiss.

"You're powerful," she continues. "But you're untrained, and you don't know how to maximize your abilities." Opening the bottom drawer of the dresser, she retrieves a pair of jeans. She slides them snugly over her thighs and bounces to pull them over her hips, buttoning them at the top. Then she puts on a sheer top and steps into a pair of combat boots. "You ready? Let's go have some fun."

"Right now? I thought we were going to talk about me trying out for the Core."

She slips on a leather biker jacket. "There are many factors to consider with a new recruit."

"Like what?"

Snatching a set of keys off the counter, Eliza heads toward the front door. "Like whether or not the recruit knows how to have fun." Her boot crunches down on shattered glass in the hallway. "We spend nearly all our time together, and I'm not going to do that with someone I can't stand."

Shutting the door behind me, I ask, "Do you want me to lock it?"

She waves me off and says, "Don't worry about it. Nobody knows it's here. We might as well be on a deserted island."

As I follow her downstairs, I ask, "What do you do for fun?"

We climb inside her shiny orange car. It still has the new car smell. Eliza revs the engine. "Whatever I want."

NINE

A valet attendant opens Eliza's car door. He hands her a ticket and gets behind the wheel. Realizing I'm still in the passenger seat, he clears his throat, signaling it's time for me to get out. As I step onto the curb, I notice the procession of vehicles behind us, whose occupants are growing increasingly more agitated the longer they have to wait. They don't strike me as belonging to a socioeconomic class that typically has to wait for anything. The women are adorned with expensive jewelry, and the men look like they drop more on weekly haircuts than I make in a month.

A velvet rope cordons off the people waiting in line at the entrance of the Mule Kick Club. I've never been here, but I recognize the exterior of the club from photos in celebrity magazines. If you're not somebody in Loganstin, you've never made it past the ropes at the Mule Kick.

Eliza walks to the front of the line. Two very large men with shaved heads stand behind the velvet rope. They wear headgear and one clutches a clipboard. "Hey, Big T," Eliza says.

The man holding the clipboard turns to her and a smile spreads across his face. "Yo, E. What's shaking?"

"Nothing yet, but hopefully that'll change," she says. "How's it in there?"

"It's bumpin'. You coming in?"

"My bumps need to bump, and that ain't gonna happen out here," she says.

Big T unfastens the velvet rope and holds it aside for Eliza and me to pass. "Get bumpin'."

This causes a chorus of grumbles from the people waiting in line, but if Eliza notices, she doesn't show it. We walk past Big T toward the door.

"Who the hell is she?" asks a man wearing a silk shirt with a dragon embroidered on it.

Big T shoots the man a glare and says, "If you knew, you'd wet yourself."

A doorman opens the front door, allowing Eliza and me to enter.

"Shouldn't we get in line?" I ask.

"Why would you if you don't have to?" she asks.

"To wait our turn."

Standing on the threshold of the club, Eliza leans in and plants a kiss on my cheek. "That's so cute." She grabs my hand and walks inside.

Techno music blares at an ear-piercing level, a thumping bass that rattles your bones. Men and women gyrate in a hedonistic mass on the dance floor. The air is musty and thick, reeking of sweat, liquor, and perfume.

I follow Eliza through the crowd of people. She cuts expertly through them, heading to the back wall where VIP tables and booths are positioned so everyone can see and be seen by everyone. And a quick glance tells me that we're being seen. A hostess sees Eliza coming and motions us toward one of the empty booths, where a *Reserved* sign sits. I scoot into the booth and Eliza slides in next to me.

The music is so loud that the hostess has to lean over the table to shout, "What would you like to drink?"

Eliza says, "A Purple Hooter."

Both ladies glance at me and I say, "A cola."

"A rum and cola," Eliza adds.

The hostess spins and heads off toward the bar.

Leaning in close to my ear, Eliza asks, "What do you think? Pretty cool, huh?"

"Do you come here—"

Before I can finish my thought, Eliza slides out of the booth. "I'll be right back."

She walks toward a group of men standing around a tall table. They're dressed in tattered jeans and untucked dress shirts, and they're smoking thick cigars. The men all take turns embracing her, apparently pleased to see her. Eliza holds court. The men surround her and laugh as she talks. One of the guys offers her a fresh drink, which she takes and samples.

The hostess comes back to our booth carrying a tray. She sets down a glass with a purple cocktail and my rum and cola. I fumble for my wallet, but she waves me off and says, "Eliza's drinks are comped."

"Oh, okay, thanks," I say.

Then the hostess sets her tray down, slides into the booth, and cozies up to me. "What's your name?" she asks.

"Marvin."

"I'm Candy. So, are you in the Core? "

"Um … no."

"Come on, you can tell me. I won't say anything."

"No, really, I'm not."

"Okay, if that's how you wanna play it," she says, rubbing her finger over her exposed neckline. "So, is Roisin your girl-friend or something?"

"No," I say. "We're … hold it. What?"

The hostess smiles and says, "Don't worry about it. It's the worst kept secret in this place. Everyone knows."

"Oh," is all I say.

Eliza hugs all the men before heading back to the booth. The hostess slides out as Eliza approaches. They exchange curt looks, and the hostess hurries off. Eliza slides in next me. "What did she want?" she asks.

"Nothing."

Eliza takes her drink and sips it. "I bet she didn't."

"Do you know that everyone here knows that you're Roisin?"

"Really?"

"That's what she told me," I say.

She shrugs. "I guess that's why they always comp me."

"You're not upset?"

"You only need a secret identity if you want to live a nor-mal life. Normal's boring," she says, sliding out of the booth. "You ready to roll?"

I scoot out behind her.

She motions to my untouched rum and cola. "You didn't touch your drink."

"Not much of a drinker."

"Why'd you order it then?"

"I ordered the cola," I say. "You ordered the rum."

"I just assumed you'd want to go all the way," she says.

Eliza takes me on a whirlwind tour of the city, hitting every reputable nightspot and some that aren't. We get fifteen-dollar drinks at the Factory, share a basket of greasy appetizers at the Owl, and she forces me onto the dance floor at Mulligan's. She mingles with people I recognize, and disappears with people who look like hardened criminals. While this is happening, I try to find secluded spots and take a seat. I people-watch until she ushers me off to the next place.

She holds my hand and leads me to a place called the Library. It's dark and smoky, and music plays softly through speakers. It's actually the quietest place we've been to all night. The loudest noise comes from the steamers frothing milk for lattes. People mill about the place or sit on plush chairs and velvet sofas, smoking cigarettes and sipping espressos. Eliza waves at a group sitting in the corner. "Hey, you," she calls, crossing toward them.

Left behind, I find a large chair and sit down. An assortment of books are scattered across the battered coffee table. I rummage through them. There's apparently no theme in this collection of books—they range from self-help how-to's to romance paperbacks.

I pick up a stained copy of a book titled *Strange Phenomenons Explained*. I open it and start reading. One of the strange phenomenons is the toppling of the city of Jericho's walls during the Battle of Jericho in the Bible. After crossing the Jordan River, Joshua led the Israelites into Canaan, where they laid siege to the city. The Lord spoke to Joshua, telling him to march around the city once each day for six days, with seven priests carrying rams' horns in front of an ark. On the seventh day, they were to march around the city seven times, after which the priests were to blow their horns. Joshua did this, commanding his people not to give a war cry until he told them to do so. After marching around the city the seventh time, the priests sounded their horns, and Joshua ordered the people to shout. The walls collapsed, and the Israelites charged straight into the city, destroying it.

The book then states that the Israelites' silent marching created a seismic wave within the city's walls. So, when they shouted to the heavens on the seventh day, it caused an acoustic shockwave, which prompted a mini earthquake. Thus explaining why the walls came tumbling down.

I don't know how much time passes before Eliza plops down in the chair across from me, but I'm on page seventy-three. "Here you are," she says. "What're you reading?"

I hold the book up and show her the cover.

"Good?" she asks.

"Yeah, it's interesting," I say.

"You like to read?"

"Yes."

"Not really my thing." Eliza lifts her feet and rests her boots on the table. "So, Marvin, what do you do for fun?"

"I hang out with my friends."

"So what do you do when you're hanging out?"

"I don't know. Go to the park. Get a bite to it eat. Just hang out."

"Wow. You guys sound really boring."

I close the book and replace it on the coffee table. "I suppose."

"We're going to have to loosen you up," Eliza says. "So, do you wanna get high?"

———

The roar of the water rushing out of the Porcupine Dam into the Loganstin River is deafening. Standing on the ledge of the concrete valve tower, I marvel at the sheer volume of water being released, watching as it settles into a violent churning pool. A black abyss. The mist is so dense that it blankets Eliza and me like a sauna, but this water is rather chilly. I shiver and zip my jacket up.

"You ready?" Eliza yells over the roaring water.

"For what?" I say.

She takes my hand and walks off the ledge. I instinctively pull away from her to avoid plummeting into the water below, but with more strength than I'd think her capable of, she pulls me with her.

Clenching my eyes shut, I prepare to drop to my death.

But something strange happens. Instead of free-falling, we move upward. I open my eyes and panic when I realize that Eliza and I are walking up the mist, like we're climbing a staircase. Or rather, Eliza is walking skyward and I'm the unwitting passenger along for the ride.

"Oh … my … god," I say.

"I told you we were going to get high." She laughs.

"You're walking on the mist?"

"Anything denser than air, and I'm good to float."

We move higher and higher until we reach the top of the mist. It's like flying through the top of a cloud. We perch there like butterflies on a leaf. The open vastness below my feet is awe-inspiring. "How am I doing this?" I ask.

She pulls her hand from mine, so that our fingertips are just barely touching. I slowly sink down through the mist, like I'm tethered to the ground and it's pulling me down. "If I pulled away my hand, you'd sink like a stone," she says.

"Then please don't pull away your hand," I say, bobbing up and down on the mist like a buoy.

Smiling mischievously, Eliza lifts her fingers so only two touch me. It feels like I'm hanging by a thread. Gravity's grip fastens around me and threatens to pull me to my death as Eliza toys with me. "Uh-oh," she says. "This isn't looking good for you."

I sink lower. The tip of Eliza's index finger is all that's keeping me from plummeting downward. I wrap my other arm around her legs, clinging for dear life. The contact with her restores my immunity to gravity. She laughs as I climb up her like a utility worker climbing a telephone pole. My face slides along the front of her body as I scurry up. Something has changed in Eliza's eyes. She pulls me in close and kisses me like she's trying to extract all my secrets. I kiss her back, as we embrace hundreds of feet in the air.

TEN

The next afternoon, Yvonne, Kent, and I sit at a table in a fancy sidewalk café. I hate this place. The portions are small, the prices are high, and the servers are rude. But Yvonne loves this restaurant, and I can't figure out why. She's sitting back in her chair, hands behind her head, basking in the afternoon sun. "I love this place," she says. "Give me one good reason why we don't come here more often."

Picking at my goat-cheese-and-beet salad, I look around at the other restaurant patrons. I'm fielding a few judgmental glances tossed my way, and I suspect that the men in suits and women in designer clothing are wondering why three teenagers in dirty jeans and faded T-shirts are polluting their favorite eatery.

"It ain't no Eat-A-Rama," Kent mutters.

"Amen," I reply.

"Shut up," Yvonne says. "I'm not going to let the two of you ruin this for me, because this is probably the last time I'll have enough money to eat here."

"Why?" I ask.

"I've got to find a real job. I'm done getting junkies high."

I don't have to ask why the sudden change of heart about using her power to make money. The junkie's daughter, Harry, really threw Yvonne for a loop.

Kent grumbles. "Not you too. Now I live with two boy scouts."

"Don't listen to him," I say. "I'm glad you decided to get a real job."

"Well, I hope you guys aren't waiting for me to go soft," Kent says.

Yvonne reaches over and pokes her finger deep into Kent's spongy flesh. "You're already soft."

He pushes her hand away. "You know what I mean. We've got abilities, and I don't think it's wrong to use them to support ourselves. Is it wrong for a bird to fly, or a fish to swim? I think not."

"I'm not telling you what to do," Yvonne says. "I'm just done doing what I've been doing. It's my decision. You can make yours."

Kent runs his fingers over his face like he's reading Braille. "How's my face holding up?"

I don't recognize this facial mold. It must be new. The face has a strong jaw line and a dimple in the chin. "How'd you get that scruff?" I ask.

"You don't want to know. How does it look?"

"Not bad," I say. "Who is it?"

"I made him from scratch. My own creation."

"Looks like Ambrose McCoy," Yvonne says.

"The actor?" Kent asks.

"Yep. Spitting image," she says.

Kent picks up the stainless steel saltshaker and looks at his reflection. "No it doesn't."

"Sorry, dude," Yvonne says, closing her eyes. "Totally does."

"What about the dimple?"

"Ambrose has one."

"He does?"

"Yep."

Kent slams the saltshaker down on the table. "That sucks. I was going for something new."

Our waiter, a guy in a vest and bow tie, saunters up to the table clutching the leather check folder against his chest like it's a prized possession. "Can I get you children anything else?"

"How about a bottle of milk and a blankie?" Kent snaps.

"Has anyone ever told you that you look like Ambrose McCoy?" the waiter says, raising an eyebrow. "Like his homeless younger brother or something."

Kent snatches the check folder out of the waiter's hands. "Don't expect a tip, dickwad."

"Believe me, one look at you guys and I already knew I could kiss off any form of gratuity," the waiter says, disappearing back inside the restaurant.

"Yvonne, we're never coming here again," Kent says, inspecting the bill. His face falls. "Are you kidding me with this check? We're for sure never coming here again." He pulls a couple bills from his pocket, stuffs them into the folder, and hands it to me.

I take one look at the check and say, "That much for a salad? What a rip-off."

"Why do I even try?" Yvonne says, straightening up. "I

go out of my way to expose the two of you to different things, and all I get is a bunch of whining. You'd think—"

An ear-piercing explosion down the street shatters the quiet afternoon. The entire face of a storefront is blown away. It rains brick and glass onto the street. The force of the shockwave overturns tables, shattering plates and glasses all over the sidewalk. A cloud of debris billows out of the newly created hole and moves toward us. Screaming people run for cover.

My friends and I huddle behind our overturned table, using it as a shield from the river of dust and debris that flows over us. "What was that?!" Yvonne yells.

Poking my head around the table, I survey the damage and see a gaping hole in the front of the adjacent building. A man in a ski mask stands on the rubble in front of the blown-out storefront. He surveys the sky before quickly disappearing inside the jagged hole.

"Who was that?" Kent asks.

"Let's go find out," I say, jumping out from behind the table.

Yvonne grabs my arm. "I don't think that's a good idea."

"I just want to see what's going on." The soles of my shoes crunch on the shattered glass and fragments of concrete as I hurry down the sidewalk. The cloud of dust is so thick I have to swat at it, like with bugs on a summer night.

"This is gnarly," Kent says, behind me. We scurry out into the street to get a better look. Dark smoke slithers like a snake from the smoldering hole. "What is that place?"

Yvonne points at our feet where a sign reads, *Kane Fine Jewelry*.

An armored truck rumbles down the street. It careens

through the damaged vehicles like a plow through snowdrifts. Then it gets stuck at a pile of rubble. The gears grind as the driver shifts into a lower gear, and the engine revs as the truck climbs over the rubble and up to the hole in the jewelry store. I watch as the back doors of the vehicle open and two men— red bandanas over their faces and clutching duffle bags— jump out and join the guy in the ski mask.

"It's a heist," Kent says.

"We've got to stop them," I say, stepping toward the smoldering wound in the side of the building.

Yvonne grabs my hand and says, "Don't!"

"Why?" I ask. "This is our chance."

"Our chance for what?"

"To do some good."

"We're not sticking out our necks and exposing ourselves," she says.

The robbers toss full bags into the back of the truck, where they land with a thud. Then the trio quickly disappears back inside the store.

"Come on. We can do this. The three of us."

My friends exchange looks. Kent shrugs and says, "Whatever."

Yvonne stomps her foot on the ground. "Have the two of you lost your minds? No. No. No. This isn't our fight."

"But it can be," I say. "Come on. Let's do it."

Shaking her head, she says, "Absolutely not. We can't take the chance."

The robbers hurry out with more bags in hand, tossing them in the back of the armored truck.

"Suit yourselves. I'll do it myself." As I head toward

the jewelry store, a red blur appears out of nowhere. Streak stops at the back of the armored truck.

"Oh, crap, hide," Kent says. "It's Streak. He might recognize us."

We take cover behind a mound of rubble, then climb over jagged concrete and bricks to the top, where we position ourselves for a better view.

"You don't think he'll remember us from the park, do you?" Yvonne asks.

"I think he's a little distracted right now," I say.

Streak zips around the three robbers. And while we don't see him hitting them, the physical effects are evident. The one wearing the ski mask is smacked off his feet and flies back, landing just inside the jewelry store. The other two robbers fly in opposite directions. One slams into the side of a parked car, while the other one crashes through the only unbroken pane of glass on the whole block.

"I think we should get out of here," Yvonne says.

"Are you nuts?" Kent says. "It's just getting good."

The red blur comes to a stop and Streak looks at the unconscious robbers. An upper section of the jewelry store dislodges and plunges to the ground just behind the crimson-clad hero. Startled, Streak jumps, and then he darts left in a blur. Arms flailing, he trips over a large piece of concrete, falls to the ground, and skids along the rubble. He comes to an abrupt stop near the three of us.

Groaning, Streak pushes himself off the ground. The entire front of his costume is shredded, revealing exposed skin that's scraped and bleeding. His arms give out and he collapses.

The sound of sirens blares in the distance, getting louder

as the emergency vehicles draw near. "Let's get out of here before the police show up," Yvonne says, making her way through the rubble.

"Do you think we should just leave him?" I ask.

Kent follows after Yvonne, saying, "Dude, he'll be fine. Come on."

The sirens get louder.

"He doesn't look too good," I say.

"Come on, Marvin," Yvonne yells.

I hesitate before chasing after my friends. As the three of us head away from the approaching sirens, I wonder whether it'll ever get any easier doing what's right.

ELEVEN

The next evening, after the dinner crowd at Midtown Café has thinned, I spot Gus behind the counter, setting a drink in front of a girl sitting on a stool. Most of the tables are empty now, and Gus sees me and waves me over. He motions to the girl. "I just hired someone."

That's when I realize the girl is Yvonne. She flashes me a smile.

"Yvonne?" I say.

"Hey," she says.

"You hired her?" I ask.

"Weirdest thing," Yvonne says. "I came in looking for you, and he just up and offered me a job."

Gus says, "She's your replacement."

"What?"

"I'm going to be a busser and dishwasher," she says.

"If she's doing that, what am I supposed to do?"

"Marvin, I need to talk to you," Gus says, stepping away from the counter. "I'd appreciate your support on this."

"But I—"

Gus raises his hand to silence me. "You and I both know that Yvonne needs this. She's trying to make a change. And she's in a delicate spot. For someone like her, if there's a little hiccup, she'll just go back to doing what she was doing before, and we don't want that, do we?"

"Did she tell you ...?"

He waits for me to finish my thought, but I hold my tongue. "Tell me what?" he asks.

"Never mind," I say. "But what about me? She's taking my job."

"You're going to wait tables. You're my new waiter," Gus says. "Well, once you've trained Yvonne."

I can't help but smile. "Really?"

"I'm giving this to you because you've worked hard and paid your dues," he says. "There are no shortcuts in life, Marvin, so don't believe anyone who tells you differently. There aren't any golden tickets. The only things worth having are those that take blood, sweat, and tears." He wraps his arms around my shoulder and gives me a friendly squeeze. "Show Yvonne the ropes."

Rejoining Yvonne, I ask, "Did you tell Gus about getting junkies high?"

Evidently not hearing me, she slides a newspaper across the counter. "Did you see the paper?"

"No," I say, picking up the broadsheet and opening it. She points to the photo on the front page. It's the jewelry store. The street is in shambles. And in the forefront, Streak is shown sprawled on the ground, lying exactly where he landed after tripping. "Yeah?"

"Look at the headline."

Splashed across the paper in big bold letters, it says *Gang of Dirties Attacks Streak!*

"There wasn't a gang of dirties there," I say.

Yvonne sips her soda. "It says that Streak was injured after battling with them. Can you believe it? What a joke."

"But it isn't true," I say.

Gus sticks his head around the corner and says, "Marvin, what am I paying you for?"

I jump up and motion for Yvonne to follow me. "Let's get you clocked in."

After I get her a timecard, we go over to the mountain of greasy pots and pans waiting to be cleaned. Filling the sink with hot water, I toss Yvonne a clean rag. I scrub the dishes and she dries them. "If you can survive doing this, then so can I, right?" she asks.

"You're going to do great." I nudge her with my hip. She nudges me back.

Once we put all the dishes away, I take her into the walk-in refrigerator and show her how to maintain the inventory and how to order items that we need. She takes one look at all the food and whistles. "Dang," she mumbles. "This would keep us fed for a year. Well, until you used your power and ate it all in one sitting."

I make sure nobody is within earshot. "You're a civilian now," I say. "You've got to act like it and be careful what you say."

Yvonne shadows me the rest of the shift, watching my every move. We wipe down the counters, stock the coolers, and clean the tables.

Everyone has left for the night with the exception of Gus, who finally emerges from his office with three Styrofoam containers. He sets them on the counter and says, "Yvonne, here are some leftovers for you. I made sure to get you some of our world-famous ribs. It's up to you whether or not you want to share them with Marvin."

She flips open the lid and the ribs are still hot, releasing sweet-smelling steam. "Um, Marvin, you can gnaw on the bones after I'm done."

"Whatever happened to seniority?"

"Seniority gets trumped by her being better-looking than you," Gus says.

"Damn straight," Yvonne says.

"Show her how to set the alarm when you leave." And with that, Gus is gone.

"He seems pretty cool," she says.

"Yeah, he's a good guy."

Motioning to the leftovers, she asks, "Are you hungry?"

"Yeah."

"Grab some napkins and let's eat."

Sliding on my belly over the counter, I get the napkins and push myself up, plopping my butt on the barstool. We eat the ribs, enjoying every greasy and saucy bite.

I glance at the clock and realize I'm going to be late. We finish eating and clean up, tossing away fistfuls of greasy napkins. "Let's arm the security system," I say.

As we step outside and shut the door behind us, I reach into my pocket and retrieve my key. "Hold up," Yvonne says, producing an identical key. "Gus gave me one."

"He did?"

She slides her key into the lock. "Yeah."

"Great. That's great."

Yvonne plops down on the bench at the bus stop, but I walk by, heading down the sidewalk. "Are we not going to take the bus?" she asks.

"You go ahead," I say. "I'll meet you at home."

She gets up. "I'll come with you."

"Um … I've got something to do."

"I'll come with."

"That's okay. You don't have to."

"I know I don't have to. I want to."

Backing away, I say, "Well, I better do this myself."

"What're you talking about?"

"Just go home. I'll see you later."

"Marvin, tell me what's going on," she says.

"Yvonne, it's nothing—"

"Is this about Gus giving me a key?"

"No, it's not about the key," I say.

"If you're upset that Gus gave me a job, I'll quit. I can find another job."

"I don't freaking care about the job or the key!" I snap.

Yvonne looks like I just slapped her. Her face falls and her jaw muscles tighten. "Okay," she says, sitting down on the bus bench. "I'll just see you later."

"Yvonne—"

"It's fine, Marvin," she says. "Don't worry about it."

My face flushes with shame. I walk down the street, turning to glance back at her. She sits there with her hands in her lap, waiting for the bus. I watch her for a moment, wondering if she'll look my way, but she doesn't.

TWELVE

Three blocks from where I left Yvonne at the bus stop, Eliza sits in her car waiting for me. I get in and she speeds away.

"Hey, you know that whole thing with Streak yesterday at the jewelry store?" I ask.

"Yeah."

"There wasn't a gang of dirties there."

"Huh?"

"I was right there eating lunch. I saw the whole thing," I say. "Streak getting hurt was just an accident. He tripped and fell. That's it."

She shoots me a look and says, "You're confused."

"No, I saw—"

"You're confused," she interrupts. "Forget what you think you saw."

We don't talk the rest of the way to the Loganstin River. There's an island in the middle of the river that houses the Core Mansion. Actually, calling it a "mansion" is unimaginative. It's a monument to power. The base of the building would be a mansion in itself, but the spiraling tower is the tallest building in the city. Gargoyles perch on the rooftop turrets, around a dancing flame that's never extinguished. It's called the "Flame of Truth." One of the most iconic photos of Loganstin ever taken is when dark clouds covered the city skyline. The top of the mansion tower was blanketed, but the Flame of Truth burned brightly through the darkness. A beacon of justice.

Stopping the car, Eliza slides open the console and presses her thumb against a scanner. A beam of light reads her fingerprint, and a mechanical voice says, "Identity verified."

A section of road emerges and expands across the river. Not waiting until this bridge is fully formed, Eliza slams the car into gear and hits the gas, speeding over the river. The bridge is incredibly narrow. Turning the wheel just a fraction of an inch would probably send us careening into the dark, cold water. As if it has a mind of its own, my foot hits the floor repeatedly, trying to slow down the car. "Could you please slow down?" I ask.

Eliza removes her hands from the wheel. "Look! No hands," she yells.

I grab the wheel and try to keep it straight. "What're you doing?!"

"Relax." She peels my hands off the steering wheel. "It's on automatic."

"Huh?"

"When a vehicle is on the bridge, it's controlled automatically."

Sitting back in my seat, I notice that the car hasn't drifted even an inch without hands on the wheel. "Oh" is all I say.

Eliza reaches out and pinches my cheek. "God, you're so cute. I could just eat you up."

We drive onto the island and head straight for the side of the Core Mansion, where the wall slides open on giant stone rollers. The car pulls inside.

The whole area is roughly the size of an aircraft hangar and looks like a showroom for exotic transportation, somewhere for people with too much money to shop. There's a tiny helicopter that looks like the aircraft equivalent of a go-cart. Resting next to it is the smallest jet plane I've ever seen, not much bigger than Eliza's car. "Do those actually fly?" I ask.

"Wouldn't do us much good if they didn't," she says.

"Who flies them?" I ask.

"Pretty much any of the Core who can't fly on their own."

"Even you?"

"I have," she says, pulling the car into a stall next to a camouflage urban-assault vehicle with rotating turret and attached machine gun. "And you'll be able to if you join the team."

"That would be tight," I say, unable to suppress the grin that spreads across my face.

We get out and I follow her toward a door. On the walk, I'm scanning the vehicles. I'm looking for one in particular. Probably the most recognizable vehicle on the planet. Eliza sees me rubbernecking, and she rolls her eyes as she points, grumbling, "It's over there."

Looking that way, I spot it: Mystic's Jet Car. It's legendary. The last three presidents have requested a ride in it. It looks like no other car. If a jet and a drag speedster had a baby, it would produce Mystic's car. "Can I touch it?" I say, admiring the pitch-black automobile.

"Really?"

"Yeah."

She sighs. "I guess. But hurry. We're already late."

The closer I get to it, the blacker it looks. It's as if it swallows light, like a black hole. I marvel at how clean it is. It's spotless. Not a water spot, a smudge, or a speck of lint. It's perfect. Extending my hand to stroke the hood of the speedster, I hesitate. What if I leave a fingerprint or scratch the paint? I couldn't live with myself. Standing there, I stare in awe at it. It doesn't seem real. If it weren't for my reflection staring back at me in the paint, I'd think I was imagining this. Mystic's Jet Car.

Next to Lieutenant Mercury, Mystic is the most revered and respected member of the Core. And she's the only member who doesn't wear a mask. There's been speculation about why she chooses not to conceal her identity, but I subscribe to the belief that it's because she's beautiful. Wearing a mask would conceal her long, golden hair that's never messed up, even after flying through the sky at supersonic speeds when hitching a ride with one of the fliers. She must use a ton of hair spray, that's all I can figure. Also, a mask would cover her perfect café-au-lait complexion, which rivals those of any of the models featured on the covers of magazines. Mystic has the power to read minds, but I don't think she has to use her powers to know what most men are thinking.

"Are you going to touch it or what?" Eliza asks.

My hand hovers above the car's hood. "I can't."

"Then come on."

"When we're done, can I get a picture of me standing next to it?" I ask.

"Marvin, if you're going to be invited to join the Core, you've got to get rid of this fanboy-type attitude. It's not cool."

"But it's Mystic's Jet Car."

"Yeah, and it gets crappy mileage and the air conditioner never works," she says. "If you get all dopey and gooey-eyed over everything, you're going to make everyone uncomfortable. You've got to chill."

"But can I still get a picture of me next to the car?"

Eliza grumbles and storms off. She places the palm of her hand against a scanner. There's a humming noise followed by a green light, which moves from the bottom up as it reads her hand. The elevator door opens and we step inside. As the door closes, I notice there aren't any floor buttons. "Basement," she says.

The elevator rapidly descends. I reach out and rest my hand on the railing to stabilize myself. "So, what's going to happen, exactly?" I ask.

"Some routine tests," she says. "Dr. Klaus will take blood and urine samples."

"Dr. Klaus?" I interrupt.

"The Core's physician."

The elevator comes to a stop and the door opens. Eliza steps out and I follow behind her, finding myself in what could be mistaken for a medieval dungeon. The dark corridors are made of stone and lit by dim electric lanterns that flicker. It smells like centuries-old mold. We make our way down the corridor, passing a series of closed doors with enormous cast-iron handles.

Eliza stops outside a door at the end of the corridor. She knocks on it, which creates an echo that bounces off the stone walls. I hear the heavy sound of footsteps approaching, and the door swings open to reveal an attractive woman in a lab coat, a skirt that's tight in all the right places, and a silk blouse that if opened one more button would be scandalous.

She pokes her head out and looks around. "Eliza, I told you to call me when you were in the garage." She motions for us to hurry inside.

Eliza takes my hand in hers and says, "Jeez, Lady, relax. Nobody saw us."

The woman hurries to close the door. "Do you know how much trouble I'll be in if anyone finds out?" She enters a code into a keypad. When she hits *enter*, a series of locks fasten and there's a hissing of air. "So don't tell me to relax."

"Marvin, this is Dr. Lady Klaus," Eliza says. "Lady, this is Marvin."

I'm struck by the room's pungent odor, which smells like antiseptic and bleach. The doctor notices my grimace. "Sorry about the smell. I just disinfected. I need a completely sterile environment to perform the tests."

Everything about the lab is sterile, including the white ceramic tiles that cover the floor, walls, and ceiling. Floodlights blanket every square inch in a harsh radiance. The room is chilly, and I'm surprised I don't see my breath. On one side of the lab, there's everything you'd expect in an operating room: monitors, a stainless-steel gurney, respirators, and a small tray on wheels where shiny metal tools are neatly arranged—tools that make me nervous. The other side of the lab houses physical therapy equipment. There's a rack with weights of varying sizes and shapes. A section of the floor has a conveyor belt that looks like a treadmill for an elephant. There's a large Plexiglas tank filled with a green, bubbling liquid. It contains a single-person seat that looks like it submerges to the bottom.

Dr. Klaus stands by the stainless-steel gurney and pats it. "If you'd please lie down here," she says. As I cross to the gurney, I step over a drain in the floor just in time to see a small trickle of light pink liquid disappear into the grate. It looks like blood. As I sit down on the gurney, Dr. Klaus says, "Oh, sorry, I need you to disrobe."

My eyes dart from the doctor to Eliza. "Like, naked?" I ask.

"Just down to your underwear."

As I remove my shirt and pants, Eliza hovers near me and takes them. She's like a mother in a dressing room with a child trying on clothes. "I need to take you shopping," she says. "Your wardrobe isn't working for me."

Feeling self-conscious in my underwear and socks, I sit on the lip of the gurney.

While inspecting forms on a clipboard, Dr. Klaus says, "Have you ever been tested?"

"Yeah," I say. "I tested dirty when I took the test after my powers started."

"No, I mean a real test," she says.

"A real test?" I repeat. "I thought that was the real test."

Dr. Klaus sets the clipboard down, pats the gurney, and says, "Lie down on your back."

The gurney is cold, and I flinch as I lie flat. The doctor stands over me as she retrieves a stethoscope from her lab coat pocket. She places the end of it against my chest. "Deep breath."

I inhale deeply and then exhale.

She moves it to the other side. "Again."

I repeat the process.

Dr. Klaus removes the listening device, smiles, and places her hand gently on my chest. "Good. Everything sounds normal for a ... how old are you?"

"What time is it?" I ask.

She looks confused. "Half past midnight."

"Then I turned eighteen thirty minutes ago."

"Happy birthday," Eliza says, bending down and planting a kiss on my mouth. Her breath is warm and sweet. "You're legal."

Dr. Klaus snickers. "Well, everything sounds normal for a healthy eighteen-year-old." She picks up a pen light from the nearby table and clicks it on. Leaning over me, she shines the light into my right eye. Satisfied, she moves to the other eye. Standing up, she turns off the light and sets the pen light back down. "So far so good."

"Are you going to get in trouble for doing this?" I ask.

The doctor opens her mouth to say something, but Eliza interrupts. "There's generally a protocol for this kind of stuff, but Lady agreed to do this for me as a favor."

"A favor?" Dr. Klaus says. "Is that what we're calling sneaking around in the middle of the night?" She peels a film off of the back of a round sticker, like a bandage, and sticks the adhesive side on my chest, over my heart.

"What's that?" I ask.

"A blood pressure monitor," she says. The monitor beeps, and Dr. Klaus leans down to read the display. "Your blood pressure is a little high." After removing the sticker and discarding it, she scribbles on her clipboard. "Eliza, will you hand me the syringe?"

Eliza steps over to the table, shuffling my clothing to free up a hand. "Which one? The little one or the big one?"

"The big one."

Eliza picks up the biggest syringe I've ever seen. The needle shimmers under the lights.

"What's that for?" I ask, trying not to sound as nervous as I am.

"A blood sample," Dr. Klaus says, taking the syringe from Eliza.

"How much blood do you need?"

She inspects the needle before moving toward the foot of the gurney, where she grabs my ankle and positions the syringe at the sole of my foot. "You might feel a slight prick," she says, right before sinking the entire needle into my foot.

I would love to be able to say I retain my composure and handle this incredible discomfort like a champ, but I can't—I howl like a sissy and thrash my head from side to side like a mortally wounded animal. When the doctor removes the needle, the syringe's enormous chamber is filled with blood. "Now, that wasn't so bad," she says.

"Yes, it was," I bark. "Why did you take blood from my foot?"

"The blood cells in an IWP—"

"IWP?" I ask.

"Individual With Powers," Eliza says.

"Anyway, if the blood isn't taken from the feet, it produces zero information. It's like running a blood test on water," Dr. Klaus says. "But for some reason, the blood taken from the foot yields information."

"Why's that?"

"Don't know for sure. It's probably due to the compromised circulation in feet, but nobody really knows."

"They didn't take blood from my foot when I tested dirty," I say.

"Those tests are total bullshit," Eliza says.

"What?"

Dr. Klaus shrugs. "There was an amendment passed to the Clean Powers Act that puts a quota on how many IWPs can be classified as clean."

"Why's there a quota?"

"It was done to curb unfair competition between people with powers and normies."

This feels more disillusioning than when I found out that Santa, the Easter Bunny, and the Tooth Fairy weren't real. I'm beginning to suspect that everything I've been led to believe about dirties is a lie.

"Trust me, it was better than some of the alternatives," Dr. Klaus says. "There were other options being considered on how to thin the herd of IWPs." She unscrews the needle and plunger from the syringe and places the chamber of blood into a cradle on the table. When she presses a button, the chamber of blood is sucked into the device. The equipment revs to life, flashing a series of lights and chirping. "This will analyze your blood and tell us what's what. Now, I need you to power up. We're going to measure your power."

"Measure my power?"

"There are categories for measuring power," Eliza says.

"It's measured on a scale from one to ten," Dr. Klaus explains. "But there are dozens of variables that determine where you might land."

"Mercury is an eight," Eliza says.

"Wait. Lieutenant Mercury is an eight? If he's an eight, who's a ten?" I ask.

Eliza picks up a syringe that has a thick blue gel inside the chamber, and, holding it up to the light, inspects it. "Actually, there's never been anyone documented as a ten. But there have been a couple of nines."

Dr. Klaus snatches the syringe from Eliza and sets it back down on the table. "There was a woman in Utah who was a nine. And do you remember a guy called Bird?"

I shake my head.

"He was a little before our time," Eliza says. "But he was a nine."

"What are you?" I ask, looking at Eliza.

"I'm a five."

"That's it?"

"Hey, being a five is nothing to be ashamed of," she says. "Mystic is a three."

"Marvin, power up so we can find out where you land," Dr. Klaus says.

Both women step back and stare at me, waiting.

"There's a problem," I say. "I need fear to power up."

The doctor writes this down on the clipboard. "Interesting. Very interesting," she says, scribbling more notes.

Eliza smirks and says, "Lady, I might've let it slip to a couple of people that you agreed to perform this test on Marvin."

I see fear rising in Dr. Klaus. Her eyes are like daggers. "What?"

Ignoring her, Eliza looks at me and asks, "How's that?"

As I feed on the doctor's fear, power courses through me.

I jump high into the air and land right behind the two women. "What do you want me to do?"

Motioning toward the conveyor belt on the floor, Dr. Klaus says, "Stand on that." I zip over to it and position myself in the middle. It jostles beneath my weight. "I need you to run on it. Start out slowly, then build to full strength. It'll measure how fast you run." I begin to jog. I remain in a stationary position as the conveyor belt moves under my feet. The doctor presses a button and a thick Plexiglas blast shield rises out of the floor, separating her and Eliza from me on the conveyor belt. Jotting notes on the clipboard, she says, "A little faster."

As I run faster, the conveyor belt begins to vibrate and groan. "Am I going to break this?" I ask.

"Streak has gotten it up to 788 miles per hour," Dr. Klaus says. I stop running, but the floor under me keeps spinning and I'm tossed like a rag doll to the floor, landing with a thud.

Eliza tries to stifle laughter. "Marvin, are you okay?"

"You can't stop running like that. You have to slowly bring it to a stop," Dr. Klaus says.

"Is Streak here? At the mansion?" I ask.

"He hasn't really left his room since the jewelry store incident," Eliza says. "Between that and getting drugged at the park, I think he's trying to avoid people."

"Oh, that reminds me," Dr. Klaus says. She pulls a folded piece of paper from her lab coat pocket and hands it to Eliza. "I ran a report and got the names of IWPs that might match the person who drugged Streak."

Eliza unfolds the paper and inspects it. "Great. Thanks, Lady."

I strain my neck to get a look at the names on the paper.

Both the doctor and Eliza turn to look at me. "Go ahead, Marvin," Dr. Klaus says.

As I get back on the treadmill and begin to run, I curse under my breath that I didn't even consider the possibility of seeing Streak here. I hope I don't bump into him. But if I do, I pray that he doesn't recognize me. More importantly, I pray that Yvonne's name isn't on that list of possible suspects. What will I do if it is? If they can link Yvonne to me, will that keep me from being extended an invitation to join the Core? I'm mad at myself for even thinking this, but still...

"You're up to 178 miles per hour," Eliza says, peering at a display. She takes the pair of earmuff hearing protectors the doctor offers her. They both put them securely over their ears.

I kick it into overdrive, digging down deep and giving it all I have. The conveyor belt whizzes faster and faster. I feel like a super-powered rodent on a running wheel. The digital display on the speedometer flashes 698. I know I can do better, so I run as fast as I can. The speedometer clicks faster, slowly ticking higher and higher. Smoke begins to rise off the conveyor belt. The smell of burnt plastic fills my nostrils. I push myself to go even faster. When the digital display clicks on 768, a large sonic boom explodes. The shockwave erupts off me. Both the doctor and Eliza grimace, but they remain unharmed behind the blast shield.

My heart feels like it's going to explode, but I keep running. The speedometer reads 787. I know I can't keep this up much longer, but I have one last spurt in me, so I spend it.

After holding the pace for a couple of seconds, which seems like forever, I gradually slow down. The speedometer is a blur as the display moves downward. Finally bringing the conveyor belt to a manageable speed, I jog casually until it comes to a complete stop. I'm out of breath. I've never run that fast in my life.

The doctor and Eliza step out from behind the blast shield. "Very impressive, Marvin," Dr. Klaus says.

"How fast did I go?"

"You topped out at 803," Eliza says.

"Faster than Streak?" I say, amazed.

"How are you feeling?" the doctor asks.

"Okay, I guess."

The doctor motions to the racks of weights and dumbbells. "Let's test your strength."

My legs are wobbly as I head toward the weights. They don't look particularly heavy. Nothing much bigger than what's sold in a sporting goods store.

"So how strong are you?" Eliza asks.

"I don't know," I admit.

Dr. Klaus motions to the smallest dumbbell on the rack and says, "Let's start with that one and move your way up. Okay?"

The smallest dumbbell is so tiny it looks like something a grandmother would use during water aerobics. "I could lift that without using my power," I say.

Both the doctor and Eliza laugh. "These weights are made from a special composite that's denser than any known metal," Dr. Klaus says. "They're extremely heavy."

Gripping the dumbbell's handle, I yank on it. She's right—this is deceptively heavy. I hoist it over my head, hold it for a beat, then drop it back onto the rack. "How much does that weigh?" I ask.

"100 pounds."

Stunned, I look at the other weights. If that little one was a hundred pounds, then the biggest one must weigh over three tons. I move up the line of weights, heaving them into the air one after the other. Then I get to one I barely manage to lift off the rack, much less over my head. Giving up, I let it clank back onto the rack. "I can't do it," I say, inspecting the palm of my hand to see if I've torn the skin.

Dr. Klaus scribbles on her clipboard. "How do you feel now?"

"I think I probably have—"

Before I finish my thought, everything goes black. My legs buckle under me and I slip into unconsciousness.

THIRTEEN

I try to raise a hand to my face, but I can't move my arms. I'm overcome with a sudden sense of dread. Sweat beads on my forehead. I try to get up, but, like my arms, my legs feel immobilized.

"Get control of yourself, Marvin," a woman's voice says, coming from somewhere in the darkness. "You're going to give yourself a heart attack."

My mouth is dry and dusty, but I manage to say, "Where am I?"

The voice responds, "In the lab."

Cutting through the endless darkness, Eliza and the doctor hover over me. I'm lying on the gurney, with a needle attached to an IV drip stuck into my arm. The liquid in the plastic IV bag empties into my body.

"I'm glad your body is accepting the supplement," Dr. Klaus says, still clutching her clipboard. "It's a special brew I made."

"How long have I been out?" I ask.

Eliza leans over me and says, "Only five minutes."

"Five minutes? Are you sure?"

The doctor removes a stopwatch attached to her clipboard and holds it up for me to see. It ticks past five minutes. "I started this once you were hooked to the IV. About five minutes ago."

"How's that possible?" I say.

"It seems that using your power takes quite a toll on you. And I'd wager that when you awake, you eat and eat and eat." Dr. Klaus taps the IV bag with the tip of her manicured fingernail. "This is like a supercharged energy drink. Gives you a kick when you need it, or a recharge when you're spent."

My head feels like it's encased in a block of cement, but all in all I feel pretty good. I sit up. "Can I get some of this stuff to go?" I ask.

"I'm afraid not," the doctor says, shaking her head. "It's powerful, and I can't be handing it out to civilians."

"Oh, well," I say. "Maybe if I'm asked to join the Core, then."

Dr. Klaus shoots Eliza a quizzical look. She shrugs. "You two sneak out of here," the doctor says. "Make sure nobody sees you. I'm going to process the data, and then we'll have a better understanding of the makeup of your power."

"What level of power am I?" I ask.

"Well, I won't know for certain until I run the battery of tests." Dr. Klaus scans her clipboard. "But if I had to guess, I'd say you're an eight while at max strength."

"I'm the same level as Lieutenant Mercury?" I say. "Dang."

Eliza smiles. "Don't get cocky, Marvin."

"Those tests weren't so bad," I say.

Making sure the doctor isn't within earshot, Eliza whispers, "Hey, I've got a birthday gift for you. It's up in my room."

We stand next to each other in the Plexiglas service elevator as it goes back up. The floors pass, one after another, until we come up to the ground floor. Eliza motions behind me and says, "Look."

The elevator continues to climb upward, revealing the vast Grand Hall below. It's all white marble—the floors, walls, and giant pillars that rise up to the ceiling like majestic redwoods reaching toward the heavens. The shine reflected off the marble is blinding. I press my face against the Plexiglas as I try to take everything in. I'm sure I look like a chubby kid gazing through the window of a candy store, mouth salivating as every last ounce of self-restraint vanishes like snow in spring. I've been given a glimpse of heaven, and I want to sear this vision into my brain so I'll remember this moment forever.

An enormous fresco adorns the ceiling. It depicts elaborate scenes of muscular men and beautiful women in flowing gowns mingling in a palace high atop a mountain. "Those are the Twelve Olympians," Eliza says, motioning up at it. "In Greek mythology, they're the gods who reside on Mount Olympus."

Surrounding the base of the mountain in the painting, a sea of men, women, and children bow their heads in reverence. "What's the deal with all the people below?" I ask.

"They're basking in the patronage of the gods." Eliza shrugs. "Hey, it's Mercury's thing."

"Do many people come to the mansion?" I ask.

"Sometimes a head of state will pay a visit, but that's not too frequent. We all kind of like having a place away from the hard glare of our public lives," she says. "And absolutely nobody but the Core is allowed on the upper levels."

"What about me?"

She flashes a devious smile. "That's why we have to be sneaky."

The elevator slows to a stop at the top floor, offering a perfect view of the fresco. As the elevator door slides open, something catches my eye. I'm staring at a figure in the painting who I assume is Zeus, the king of the gods who oversees the universe. He's perched on a throne. But even the bushy white beard and hair can't disguise Lieutenant Mercury's blue eyes.

Eliza stands in the doorway of the elevator, holding her hand against the frame to keep it from closing. Following my gaze, she says, "Mercury thinks he's Zeus."

"Where are you in this mural?"

"I don't want to be painted up there until the day I'm the one sitting on the throne." She peeks out of the elevator, checking to make sure nobody is around.

Whispering, I say, "If we're going to get in trouble—"

She silences me with a finger to her lips. I try to keep up as she scurries down the hall. Motioning to a large door with elaborate engravings in the wood, she says, "That's our fearless leader's room."

Instinctively, I take a step back. My breathing quickens and I become lightheaded. Dizziness overtakes me. It feels like my legs are going to give out from under me. I stagger forward and reach out, but when I realize that I'm actually going to touch Lieutenant Mercury's door, my hand recoils. It would be like manhandling a priceless piece of art hanging in a museum.

Eliza shoves me and yells, "BOO!"

My face smacks hard against the door.

She howls with laughter. She can barely contain herself. "You should've seen your face. Classic."

From the other side of the closed door, a booming voice says, "What?!"

Grabbing my hand, Eliza pulls me away. "I thought he was gone."

"Lieutenant Mercury?" I say.

We race to a closed door farther down the hall. She pulls a key out of her pocket.

Behind us, Mercury's door is being unlocked, which sounds like Saint Peter opening the pearly gates.

Eliza fumbles to slide the key into the lock.

I watch in horror as Mercury's doorknob slowly turns.

Eliza swings the door inward.

The door down the hall cracks open.

Right as she pushes me into her room, I hear, "Eliza, what's going on?"

She responds with, "Nothing."

There's a stretch of silence, as if the man who's the greatest hero to walk the earth is trying to figure out what's really going on, sensing that something isn't quite right. I curse myself for getting into this situation. I consider stepping out into the hall and coming clean with Mercury.

"Try to keep it down, for fuck's sake," Mercury's voice booms. His door slams.

Eliza hurries into her room and locks the door. "Oh man, he almost caught us," she says.

"He swore."

"Huh?"

"Lieutenant Mercury swore," I repeat.

"And?"

"I don't know. He's just so ... I just wouldn't think he'd swear."

"Oh boy, you've got it bad," Eliza says, toggling through the music library on her MP3 player.

"Got what bad?"

"Hero worship."

"No I don't." But this denial sounds hollow to my own ears.

Finding the song she wants, she presses *play* and turns up the volume. I don't recognize the song, but the singer sounds a lot like the front man of my favorite band.

"Who is this? It sounds like Schluffer," I say.

"It sounds like them because it is them."

"I've never heard this song before."

"You like Schluffer?"

"I love them."

"This song's going to be on their next album, which I think drops in August."

"How'd you get your hands on it?"

"They heard I was a fan," she says, "so they sent me a couple of their new tracks."

Eliza's room had to have been professionally decorated. Everything from the paint to the bed skirt to the fish in the aquarium are color-coordinated and corresponding. The chrome stereo is positioned perfectly to shimmer under the soft lighting. The framed photos on the walls are hung to draw your eyes seamlessly from one to another. The entire room strikes me as a giant jigsaw puzzle, and every minute detail fits together to create a larger, grander picture.

"What do you think?" Eliza asks.

"It's great."

She retrieves a photo album and sits down on the bed, patting the spot next to her. "Come here. Look at this." I sit down, my backside sinking into the feather bed.

Opening the album and pointing out various pictures, Eliza says, "That's me with the president of Sudan. And that person I'm hugging is the heavyweight boxing champ of the world." She flips the pages, revealing a parade of pictures of herself with a variety of actors, heads of state, and athletes.

"You know a lot of famous people."

"One of the perks of being a member of the Core," she says. "You'll get to hobnob with people like this if you become a team member."

"Do you really think I'll be asked to join?"

"If you do what I tell you, then you've got a pretty good shot."

"But why me?"

Closing the photo album, Eliza leans over and rests it on the floor. She brushes my bangs out of my eyes. "You're great, and you don't even know it."

"I don't know about that," I say.

She grabs my face with both hands. "I want you to say, 'I'm great.'"

"Come on."

"Say it."

"Eliza—"

"Say it!"

"I'm … great," I mumble.

"Like you mean it."

"I'm great."

"Louder."

"I'm great!" I shout.

"Perfect," she says, still holding my face. "You're perfect." She pulls me to her and kisses me on the mouth. It's a long, wet kiss.

"Um … you didn't have to get me a birthday gift," I say, wiping my mouth.

"I wanted to."

I look around the room. "Where is it?"

Eliza kicks off her shoes and crawls to the middle of the bed, resting her head on the pillow. "It's me," she says, the smile on her face like polished veneer.

I've just been given the keys to the kingdom, and it scares the shit out of me. I'm smacked with an overwhelming wave of self-doubt, a fear that I'm not worthy and I don't belong here. I jump to my feet. "Eliza, I … this is … great. But I think I should get out of here."

"Marvin, come here."

I hesitate for a moment.

"Please come here," she says, her voice thick and syrupy.

Walking around to the side of the bed, I sit down on the edge of the mattress.

"Closer."

I feel like a fly being baited to enter a Venus flytrap. When I do, the flower will lock down on me and I'll never to be seen again. I scoot toward her.

"Lie down."

Doing as I'm told, I lie down, resting my head on the pillow next to hers.

"You need to relax," Eliza says. "You're safe with me. I know what I'm doing."

"I just—"

Before I can finish my thought, she sits up and straddles me. She grabs my hands and pins them above my head. "Don't you like me?" she asks.

Staring into her eyes, I feel small and vulnerable.

She bends down and kisses me deeply. I wrap my arms around her and kiss her back.

———

We ride down the elevator in silence. The door opens to the garage and we head toward her car. "Do you still want that photo next to Mystic's car?" Eliza asks.

"Are you sure?"

She pulls out her camera phone and holds it up. "No trouble. Got a camera right here."

I cross my arms across my chest and try to look as if standing next to Mystic's Jet Car is the most natural place in the world for me to be at this particular moment in time. Eliza snaps the photo. She inspects the image and smiles. "Done."

I continue to stare at the black car for a moment and wonder how I got here. Never in my wildest imagination had I ever dared to dream of this moment.

The two of us get into her car and she starts it, turning up the heater. As the car warms up, she runs her fingers through her hair. She wipes the corners of her mouth with her fingers, puts the car in reverse, and backs out of the parking spot.

We ride across the bridge. I stare absently out the window at the dark waters below. I feel her staring at me.

"Don't be that guy," she says. "Getting all awkward."

"Oh, I'm not," I say.

"Uh-huh."

"No, really. It's cool."

"You sure?" she asks.

"Absolutely."

"I don't want this affecting our working relationship."

"It won't."

"If everything goes as planned, we're going to be working closely together," Eliza says. "I want us to be a fit."

It's late, and the roads are empty. A light rain comes down. She turns on the windshield wipers. I listen to the sound of them going back and forth, keeping beat like a metronome. I feel that I should say something, but I'm at a loss for words. We've gone too long without talking to say something now. It would just seem strange, so I keep quiet.

Eliza drives across the Edinger Avenue overpass and pulls into the Eat-A-Rama parking lot. "Are you sure you want me to drop you off here?"

"This is fine," I say. I lean toward her to give her a kiss, but she moves to check her reflection in the rearview mirror. I don't know if this was purely coincidental or a preemptive move to avoid being kissed. I get out of the car and stand in the rain.

"Later," she says.

"Yeah, okay ... see you later," I say, shutting the door.

I watch as the car drives away, the taillights fading as they disappear from sight. A breeze sends a shiver through my body. I flip the hood of my jacket up over my head and stuff my hands in the pockets. I realize that I was subjected to two tests tonight—the doctor's, and Eliza's. If I had to guess, I'd say Eliza's carries more weight with my prospects of joining the Core.

FOURTEEN

I don't sleep a wink. I lie in bed and wonder why my room suddenly feels so small and cold. I've never thought this before, but it's like a crypt. This is what it must feel like to be dead. I finally get up and get dressed, thinking how nice it would be to have a room like Eliza's. Lots of room, light, and windows to let in fresh air.

There's absolutely nothing to eat for breakfast, so I head over to the Gas 'n' Sip, taking along my dirty laundry to wash next door at the coin-operated Laundromat. When I step out of the Gas 'n' Sip double doors—an ICEE in one hand and a bulging garbage bag of clothes in the other—I see Eliza waiting for me in her car.

"What're you doing here?" I ask.

She sits behind the wheel, resting her chin on the open window. "Looking for you."

"How'd you know I'd be here?"

She motions to the garbage bag. "Whatcha got in the bag?"

"Dirty laundry," I say. "I'm heading to the Laundromat."

"Let me save you some time. Toss the bag in the garbage."

I chuckle and nervously slurp on the ICEE.

"No, I'm serious." She points at a garbage can. "In there."

"Why would I toss out my clothes?"

Eliza starts the car and guns the engine. "We're going to get you some new ones. It's your second birthday gift."

"You don't need to spend any money on me," I say.

She pulls a credit card out of her pocket and holds it up. "I'm not. Mystic is."

"She gave you her credit card to buy me clothes?"

"No, I stole her credit card to buy you clothes."

"Is that the smartest thing to do? Can't she read minds? Won't she know what you did?"

Revving the engine, Eliza says, "Mystic can't read my mind. Let's go."

I take a final, noisy slurp of the ICEE and toss the empty cup into the garbage. As I'm about to toss my dirty clothes, I notice a bum under the awning, escaping the bright sun. "Hey, you want some clothes?" I ask. "They need to be washed, but they're in good shape."

It takes a moment for him to respond, but he eventually nods his head and I hand him the garbage bag. He opens it and rifles through the contents. Without looking up at me, he waves his thanks.

"No problem," I say, turning and getting into Eliza's car.

As she puts the car in reverse, she says, "What was that all about?"

"I gave the guy my clothes."

She rolls her eyes. "You're such a Boy Scout." The tires squeal as she speeds out of the parking lot. "We don't have time to help every little old lady across the street or get cats out of trees. The time it takes to do that willy-nilly shit, we could be doing something bigger, something that can change the world. Do you understand?"

"Yeah, I guess." I consider asking whether she'd rather I'd simply thrown the clothes away, but I stop myself—not because I'm afraid to ask but because I'm leery of her answer.

There's a three-block-long stretch of stores and boutiques in Loganstin where the wealthy go to shop—Treimel Drive. If you don't look like someone who makes a mid-six-figure income, you won't even be allowed to set foot in the stores. Rumor has it that cleans are hired as security to protect the patrons and guard the expensive merchandise. I don't know if that's true or not, but it wouldn't surprise me one bit.

Eliza and I stroll down the sidewalk. She peers into the windows, oohing and aahing at the displays of the latest couture fashions. Taking me by the hand, she pulls me into one of the stores.

We're immediately greeted by two women who have their hair pulled back so tightly that their foreheads are stretched taut, positioning their eyebrows nearly to the crest of what would be a normal person's hairline.

"Eliza, it's so nice to see you again," the one with black hair says, hugging Eliza and making the motion to kiss her on both cheeks, but not actually planting lips to skin.

"Marta, you look lovely," Eliza says.

"What can we do for you?" the other asks, embracing her, too.

"I have an emergency, Brett." Eliza motions to me and asks, "Can you do something with this?"

Trying not to stare, I steal a peek at Brett and realize that her eyebrows are actually drawn on. The women's faces pucker as they inspect me like a piece of furniture that needs to be reupholstered. "Oh my, my, my," Brett mutters.

"We can help," Marta says. The two women usher me away. "Give us some time."

"Take all the time you need," Eliza says.

I'm escorted into a dressing room. But it's not like any dressing room I've ever been in. There are no changing stalls. It's just a big, open, circular space with lights that simulate natural lighting. The rounded walls are covered with floor-to-ceiling mirrors, and there's a platform in the middle of the room.

The women proceed to remove my clothing, pulling my shirt over my head and pulling down my jeans. As I stand there in my underwear, they handle my clothes like rotten food, bundling them up and tossing them into the trash.

"Please stand on the platform," Marta says, motioning to it. I gingerly step onto it. She flips a switch, and the platform slowly spins around, rotating me like a rotisserie chicken. They study me.

"He's warm," Brett says.

"You think?"

"Absolutely. Look at his golden skin. Warm."

Marta steps forward and squints. "Yes, I suppose you're right. Clear or muted?"

Brett taps the tip of her fingernail against her front teeth. Click. Click. Click. "That's tougher. Hard to say."

Marta takes a step forward and peers at me as I slowly spin around. "He's clear," she says.

"Marta, you're right!" the other says, clapping her hands eagerly. "He's spring."

The ladies hurry out of the room. "We've got work to do," Brett says in a singsong voice.

I'm left alone, spinning around on the platform. "Am I supposed to wait here?" I call. Nobody answers me. I'm left to spin, accompanied only by the dull hum of the platform motor.

The next hour is an endless parade of shirts, pants, belts, and shoes. I try on a shirt, but that requires me to put on three different pairs of pants. And once that's settled, I slip on shoe after shoe. Brett and Marta approach buying clothes like playing chess—each move requires another calculated one, followed by another and another. It's a tireless process not for the faint of heart.

Eliza watches from a leather recliner that's rolled into the room. She sips champagne from a crystal flute and nibbles on cheese, crackers, and olives. "Eliza, what do you think?" Marta asks. I'm wearing an outfit that was twenty minutes in the making.

Eliza sips her champagne and gets up to inspect me. She nods her head, signaling her approval. "I like it," she says. Her nose crinkles. "But do you have a different color belt than that hideous brown?"

Brett unfastens the belt and removes it from around my waist in one seamless motion. "We'll be right back." She exits the dressing room with Marta.

"How much longer?" I ask.

"Oh come on," Eliza says, draining the last of her drink. She twirls the glass between her fingers. "This is fun."

I look at myself in the mirror. The cost of the clothes I'm

wearing is more than I'd like to think about. Eliza rests her chin on my shoulder and slips her arms around my waist. "Eliza, I'm not really down with all of this," I say.

"Why?"

"It's just not my thing."

"But it looks good on you," she says.

"It doesn't fit."

"What doesn't?"

"The whole thing," I say.

"But these clothes are so nice," she says. Our eyes meet in the reflection of the mirror. She sees something in them and says, "We're going out on official business."

"What?"

"We're going to follow up on the leads on IWPs that Klaus gave me. Hopefully one of them will end up being the person who drugged Streak."

A lump sticks in my throat, but I mange to croak, "Are you serious?"

"You're coming with me." Eliza pours herself another glass of champagne and says, "It's about time we pop your cherry."

FIFTEEN

We drive through Little Saigon, across Little Italy, and into Little Armenia. All the storefronts are decrepit and rundown. Eliza drives slowly, and she's either scanning the street or making sure we're seen. I can't tell for certain.

She motions to a couple of young men tossing each other hand signs from opposite sides of the street. "Those are gang signs. They're saying that you and me, we're trouble. They're warning their peeps to step aside and let us pass."

"How do they know?"

"They can sense danger," she says. "But they're just your garden-variety lowlifes peddling dope and fake IDs. They're minnows. We're after the whales."

We drive past a black guy with a shaved head who leans casually against a chain-link fence. He wears sweatpants with elastic cuffs that cling securely around his ankles. While I can't see his eyes behind the sunglasses, I feel his hard stare.

"See that guy?" she says. "The bald eagle trying to act innocent? Guaranteed he's got nearly a pound of dope in his pants."

"Aren't we going to stop him? Pick him up or something?" I say.

"His name's Chester Magnolia," she says. "Ran with the Izzy Chocolates, a syndicate rooted in the East Coast."

"The dirty gang?"

"You've heard of them?"

"Yeah," I say. My morbid curiosity makes me stare at the guy like he's a deadly accident on the side of the road.

"When he was thirteen, he got shipped to UTM."

"The supermax prison?"

"Normally that's a one-way ticket," she says. "But I got him sprung, and he works for me now. He goes about business as usual, but he lets me know when a whale is in the harbor."

The guy points his finger at me like it's a gun. He smiles as he mimics firing it at me.

"There's always going to be someone stronger and faster," she says, "so we've got to be smarter."

"Is school in session?" I ask.

"Goddamn right it is. When I'm done with you, you're going to have earned a PhD. Being a member of the Core ain't all glamour and photo ops. You gotta be willing to do a lot of grunt work. You good with that?"

"Absolutely."

She fiddles with the temperature control and adjusts the vent near me to blow on her. "I've personally been responsible for the arrests and convictions of thirty assholes, and the majority of those arrests were made when I was naked."

"Excuse me?"

She smiles and says, "'Naked' means going out as a civilian. No costumes, no powers. Naked."

My cheeks flush. "Oh."

"You dirty dog," she says. "I know what you were thinking."

I clear my throat and tug on my collar.

"As of right now, the clock's ticking for you. You've got to show me that you want this and will go to any lengths to get it," she says.

"Sounds good."

"Today you're going to get a crash course in the reality of the world we patrol, and it ain't the candy-ass world they present on those tabloid television shows."

I realize that this isn't the proper moment for me to wear a cheesy grin, but I can't help it. The more I try not to smile, the wider it grows. My cheek muscles actually start to hurt. "I'm ready," I say.

Eliza's brows furrow as she glances at me. I put a hand to my face and try to rub the smile from it, like I'm removing a stain from a garment. She turns her hard gaze back to the road. "You think you're ready? We'll see," she says.

As we head farther into Little Armenia, a sound like clapping thunder rips through the sky. I look up and instead of a bolt of lightning, I see a flier zooming into the horizon.

"Who is it?" Eliza asks, straining to spot the flier.

"I can't tell."

"Whoever it is should know better than to go supersonic within the city limits. I freaking hate fliers. Think they're so superior and above it all. Idiots."

We turn down a street that resembles photos of a war-ravaged city. Burned-out cars are discarded on the asphalt like carcasses of slaughtered buffalo on the range. There are more condemned buildings than not, and the ones that aren't probably should be.

"Where are we going?" I ask.

Eliza produces the paper Dr. Klaus gave her. "To the first name on the list."

I try to sneak a peek at the names written on the paper, but she stuffs it into her pocket. "Who are they?" I ask.

"Just a handful of dirties. A bunch of nobodies," she says. "But the first name is someone I know. So he's our first stop. He isn't our man, but I like busting this guy's balls and reminding him who's boss."

"How do you know he didn't do it?"

"McKay is a reptile who eats his young, but I seriously doubt he has the nuts to make a move against a member of the Core."

We come to a storefront on a warehouse, where a sign hanging over the door reads *McKay's Septic Sucker*. The paint outside is cracked and sun-faded. The windows are so grimy that it's impossible to see inside. Eliza presses the doorbell. Not hearing whether or not the doorbell rang, she presses it again, followed by a kick for good measure.

A muffled voice yells, "Hold on! Hold on! I'm coming already!" From the other side of the door comes the sound of a series of deadbolts being unlocked. When the door opens a crack, a pair of eyes peers at us through a security chain that's still attached. "Whaddya want?"

"McKay, open the freaking door," Eliza says.

"Eliza?"

"In the flesh."

The eyes dart from Eliza to me and back again. The door

slams shut, the chain is unfastened, and it opens wide, revealing the roundest man I've ever seen. I can't stop staring. He's as round as a snowman, with a perfectly round head, torso, and legs. "Hurry up if you're coming in," he says.

Eliza and I step inside and are immediately hit with a flood of noxious fumes, the most god-awful stench I've ever smelled. You know how when you smell something horrible, it loses its potency after a while? Well, the smell in McKay's doesn't slacken with time. It's a tour de force of grossness that never wanes.

McKay slams the door shut and refastens all the deadbolts and locks. A septic truck with a huge tank rests in the middle of the warehouse. An assortment of hoses caked in filth is coiled on the floor. "Follow me," he says, waddling past us. He perches on two stools in order to sit, resting a butt cheek on each one, the metal groaning under the weight. "Sit."

Eliza makes a face as she inspects the filthy chairs. "I'll stand, thank you very much."

"I've been hearing rumblings that there's gonna be a move made on Darren," McKay says. He raises his ample man-boob and scratches under it. A satisfied expression spreads across his face.

"Is that so?" Eliza says.

"He's had his hand deep in the cookie jar for too long. Only so long people gonna put up with that."

She rolls her eyes. "There are always going to be complainers. Nothing new."

"One of these days somebody is going to knock that guy off his pedestal, and my only hope is that I'm around to see it," McKay says.

"Nobody has the balls to make that move," Eliza says.

McKay's hand nearly disappears inside the crevices of his fat rolls as he scratches himself like a dog. "I'm guessing this isn't a social call."

"No."

"What are you going to try and pin on me this time?" he asks.

"McKay, you're so cynical," Eliza says.

He glares at her.

She produces the piece of paper and waves it around like a flag. "Your name came up on a list."

"Of course it did."

"Where were you a week ago?"

"Can you be a little bit more specific?"

"September 10th around noon."

"Why? What happened?"

"That was the day Streak was drugged in the park."

McKay settles back on the stools and chuckles. His excess body envelops them like muffin tops spilling over onto a pan. "Yeah, I read about that. But it wasn't me. I was out on a job that whole day."

"Are you sure?" Eliza says.

He glares at her. "Honey, the only thing I've ever been sure about is that right after I ate my first egg, I was sure that I would do it again." A forked tongue emerges from his mouth but disappears almost immediately, making me question whether or not I saw what I think I saw.

"That's disgusting," she says.

Without warning, McKay jumps up from the table and rushes over to the septic truck, waddling like a penguin. He grabs a hose that's attached to the tank and carries it to a kiddie pool, the small plastic kind you buy at drugstores during the summer. He squeezes the nozzle and brown waste shoots into the plastic pool. More of the gunk lands on the ground than in the pool, but McKay manages to fill it. Dropping the hose, he digs both hands into his neck as if trying to grab his tonsils through the flesh and fat. Then there's a loud snap, followed by a hissing noise as a crack appears in his head and spreads down the front of his body. He opens the crack, pulling the flesh apart to reveal a green and scaly body. The scales ripple, opening and closing as McKay breathes like gills on a fish.

"What the hell?" I say, taking three steps back.

Removing the outside body, which drops to the ground like discarded clothing, the newly revealed lizard arches its head back and stretches, shooting its forked tongue into the air repeatedly. The green beast looks rather menacing standing on its two hind legs—like a Komodo dragon, but larger and scarier.

"McKay, we don't have time for this," Eliza says. "We're in a hurry."

Ignoring her, the lizard slithers into the kiddie pool, circling around on all fours like a dog spinning around on its bed. It wallows in the brown waste, nudging it with its snout. It spins some more, going faster and faster until it stops, sticking its rear into the waste. It hisses loudly.

"Jesus!" Eliza snaps. "You couldn't have waited to do this? Way to keep it classy, you stupid iguana."

"What is it doing?" I ask.

"He's laying eggs."

I watch in horror as white eggs emerge from the lizard's rear end and plop into the waste.

"Oh. My. God," I say.

Finishing its task, the lizard inspects the dozen or so gleaming white eggs lying in the sludge. Its tongue flicks out and touches each and every egg, cleaning them off. Satisfied, it slides out of the pool, leaving its eggs behind. Slithering over to the discarded body, it begins the process of putting it back on, struggling with it like a surfer putting on a wetsuit. It notices us staring and says, "What? Haven't you ever seen a guy lay eggs before?"

"When you said that you eat your eggs, do you mean those eggs?" I say.

"Don't knock it until you try it," McKay says.

I don't know if his admission makes me more disgusted or mortified. My human sensibilities can't wrap my mind around this.

Sealing the body suit, McKay glares at us. "I'm not the dirty you're looking for. I wish I was the one who dropped Streak, but it wasn't me."

"Any ideas who it might be?" Eliza asks.

McKay waddles over to a cabinet, opens a drawer, and removes a jar of bugs covered in plastic wrap. Tossing back his head, he pours the bugs into his mouth. A handful of the tiny creatures cling to the glass, but McKay's tongue shoots out and snaps them up. I hear the sound of the bugs screeching, followed by crunching as McKay chomps his teeth down on them.

"You might wanna track down Chrome and Silver," he says.

"The twins?"

"Yeah. That sounds like something they might do."

Eliza inspects the list of names on the piece of paper. "Do you know who Yvonne McCalmon is?"

My heart skips a beat. I feel Eliza look at me, but I take great pains to turn my face away from her. I'm afraid that she'll take one look at me and put two and two together.

McKay uses his dirty fingernail to pick remnants of bugs out of his teeth. "Nope. Never heard of her." A bug crawls out of his mouth, doing its best to escape death. He pushes it back in, grinding the poor insect into wet pulp.

"So, McKay, what're you up to these days?" Eliza asks.

"I'm completely legit."

"Is that so?"

"Yeah."

Eliza scans the warehouse, taking her time, like she's studying a puzzle and working at putting all the pieces together. "Let's hope so, for your sake. Because if you're not paying the toll, you'll make a lot of people angry."

Something resembling a growl builds deep down inside of McKay. It rumbles like the sound of distant thunder. Through clenched teeth, he says, "Little girl, are you threatening me?"

"I don't make threats," she says.

McKay and Eliza glare at each other, locked in a war of wills where the first one to blink loses.

"I paid my dues in full back in Belize," he says.

"Belize? That was a lifetime ago," she says.

"It was two years ago," he says. "We're square. And the two of you should get the hell out. I've got things to do."

With the effortless grace of a gazelle bounding through

the Serengeti, Eliza makes her way over to McKay. She gets right up in his face. "Listen up, you salamander-faced ass maggot. I don't give a shit about Belize. That episode changes nothing. All I have to do is say the word and I'll have a new pair of reptile-skinned shoes."

McKay's tongue flicks out of his mouth and nearly touches Eliza's cheek. She shoves him, sending him toppling to the ground. His arm accidentally hits an egg, cracking it. Red and yellow fluid oozes out, running over his hand.

"My egg!" McKay yells. He flounders on the ground, trying to build enough momentum to rock onto his stomach and get up. It reminds me of a turtle trapped on its back.

Eliza grabs my hand and pulls me toward the door. "Let's go."

As she unlocks the deadbolts and security chains, McKay rolls back and forth. "I'm gonna kill you, you little bitch!"

We step outside. The last thing we hear before slamming the door is McKay howling, which sounds more animal than human.

SIXTEEN

I feel dirty when I get home and take a long shower, lathering up three separate times and rinsing off in scalding water. When I walk back to my room, there's a note resting on my pillow. I pick it up and see Kent's horrible handwriting. It's hard to decipher, but I manage to piece it together: *Meet me at school.*

I pass the living room on my way out. "Hey," Yvonne's voice calls out to me. She sits up and rests her chin on the back of the sofa. "How are you?"

"Good."

"Are you sure?"

"Yeah."

"You were kind of strange after work last night."

"Yeah, sorry. I've kind of got some stuff going on right now."

"What's her name?"

"What?"

"Do you like her?"

I don't know what to say, so I just stand there awkwardly, feeling like a student being interrogated in the principal's office.

Yvonne makes a face and says, "What's so complicated about liking someone or not?"

"I don't know, you tell me," I say.

"You're heading out again?"

I hold up the note. "Kent wants me to meet him at school."

We stand there looking at each other.

"Well, happy birthday," she says, turning away from me and flipping the channel on the television, signaling the end of our little chat.

The Loganstin Central High School football team hasn't won a game this season. This being the last game of the year, hopes are high that the team can avoid a sweep. But when the opposing team receives the opening kickoff and promptly runs it all the way down the field for a touchdown, the promise of victory on the Loganstin side bursts like a hard-tossed water balloon. Even the cheerleaders have lost interest, rarely turning their heads to the gridiron. Plopping down on the ground, the girls talk amongst themselves, giggling and flipping their hair away from their faces.

A handsome boy, lean and long, walks confidently toward the cheerleaders. One of them, a blonde with bright red lipstick, spots the boy approaching. Her face lights up. Her friends follow her stare and giggle as the boy walks up to them. The boy apparently says something funny, because the cheerleaders laugh like he just told the best joke ever. The blond girl gets up and walks off with the boy. Their bodies touch as they walk side by side, and the cheerleader seems to curl up against him. The couple strolls under the bleachers.

I hope Kent hurries up and makes his move. He won't have much time before his molded face loses its shape.

Kent periodically pours himself into zone-compression underwear, which is just a fancy way of saying that he stuffs himself into a girdle. The restrictive undergarments keep his body in shape, kind of like how chunky people try to appear slim. The displacement of his hefty body mass makes him three inches taller—a bonus, of course—but he says he has a hard time breathing because it's so tight. But he sucks it up, both literally and figuratively, and molds his face. He then cruises for girls, hitting school dances, sporting events, and local hangouts. Kent usually has an hour or so to pick up a girl and try to get to second base before he loses control of the flesh around his face, which is an immediate deal-breaker. He's like Cinderella at midnight—the magic disappears and everything goes back to normal, or as normal as it's ever going to get for Kent.

A shriek comes from beneath the bleachers. I race down the stairs and hurry along the front of the stands. The teary-eyed and terrified blonde passes me. Under the aluminum seating, I spot Kent glumly heading away from the football field.

"Kent," I say, running to catch up to him.

His face is sagging like a wrinkly dog. "Hey, Marvin."

I follow him toward the darkened school. "Do you want to go grab a bite to eat or something?" I ask.

"I wanna go into the school." Kent glances around to make sure nobody is watching, then tugs on the door. It's locked. He cups his palm over the lock, and his hand dissolves over it like cheese over chips. The liquid moves into the lock. There's a clicking sound, and he turns his wrist counterclockwise. The liquid oozes back out, reshaping into his hand. He tests his fingers, wiggling all five, then tugs on the door again. It opens wide and he motions me inside. "After you."

I hesitate before stepping through the open door.

The building is dark and still. The trophy case has an assortment of awards for athletic and academic achievements, with photos of students from decades past.

"Do you do this often?" I ask. "Break into the high school?"

"Sometimes."

We walk down the hall. There's a computer lab, and the door is open. I pop my head inside. "Do you think it's okay if I use a computer?" I ask.

"Who's going to care?" Kent says. "You're not going to get in any more trouble than you would for breaking and entering."

I sit down at one of the computers and jostle the mouse. The monitor turns on. I click on the Internet browser, type in "McKay+Belize," and hit *enter*.

"What're you looking up?" Kent asks.

I didn't realize he was right next to me. "Um … nothing."

The search results come up. There's not much. I scroll through the pages and finally see the link to a Spanish-language newspaper. I click on the link. The article pops up on the screen.

"You don't speak Spanish, do you?" Kent asks.

"No."

I don't recognize a word in the entire article. I scroll to the bottom and find one photo. There are five men in uniform struggling to restrain an enormous lizard—McKay. They have ropes around his neck and legs and are trying to pull him toward a police van. There's a large crowd of onlookers watching in horror.

Kent leans in over my shoulder. "I remember that. This giant lizard murdered an entire cartel in Mexico or somewhere."

"Belize."

"Yeah, that's it," Kent says. "Belize. Tore them all to shreds. Grisly. Millions and millions of dollars in drugs vanished."

"Really?"

I'm about ready to close out of the browser, but something in the photo catches my attention. I zoom in on it. The image is grainy, and she's standing far back in the crowd, but Eliza is there. She's watching McKay being led away. She looks like an American tourist, in a tank top and shorts. There's nothing about her appearance that's out of the ordinary—certainly nothing to suggest that she's a member of the Core.

"Kent, if I tell you something, you have to promise me that you won't say anything to Yvonne."

"Okay," he says.

"No, dude, I mean it," I say. "You've got to swear on your life."

"All right. I swear on my life. What's going on?"

"I met a member of the Core."

Kent dismisses me with a wave of the hand. "Right."

"I'm serious."

"Who?"

"Roisin."

He stares blankly at me, then starts massaging his sagging face. "You're not joking?"

"No."

"You're being serious?"

"Yes."

"How the hell did that happen?"

"She tracked me down after I saved that family." I point to the screen. "That's her."

Kent leans in and looks at the photo. "She's cute."

I log off of the computer and stand up. "Yeah."

He follows me into the hall, bouncing behind me like an excited dog. "Dude, what's she like? Have you met anyone else? Can I meet her? Bring her by the pad."

"If you could try out for the Core, would you?"

He stops in his tracks. "Are you trying out for the Core?"

I shush him, which I immediately feel stupid for doing because there's nobody around.

"Oh, shit, you are!" he says. "That's freakin' awesome!"

"Kent, seriously, keep it down. I'm not supposed to tell anyone."

"Does Yvonne know?"

It feels like hundreds of pins stab my stomach at the same time. I hear Eliza's voice in my head asking McKay if he knows Yvonne McCalmon, reading that name off her list of possible suspects.

"No, Yvonne doesn't know," I say.

"I'm really stoked for you," Kent says. We stand there a minute in the dark staring at each other, apparently neither one of us knowing what to say next. Kent's smile slowly fades from his face and his shoulders hunker forward like an old man's. He shuffles into a dark classroom. I stand in the doorway as my friend sits down at a desk in the middle of the room. In the darkness, he looks like just another normal teenager. But he's not. I know it, and he knows it. Kent will never be normal.

I take a seat next to him. "Are you okay?"

"I have no idea what I'm going to do with my life," he says.

"You'll figure it out."

He scoffs. "What the three of us have now is as good as it's going to get for me. And it can't last forever."

I want to tell Kent that he has a bright future. I want to tell him that the world is going to open up to him like a flower. I want to tell him that he can do anything that he puts his mind to.

But I don't. I can't. I respect him too much to lie.

He nudges me in the shoulder and says, "I'm thinking about saving up to have DNA modification. Become normal."

A flashlight clicks on and shines into the classroom. "What're you kids doing in here?" a gruff voice says. The beam of light is in my eyes, and all I can see is a silhouette of a man standing in the doorway. The dozen keys hooked to his belt jangle as he steps into the room. "How'd you get in here?"

Kent gets up and raises his hands. "We were—"

The flashlight moves from me to Kent, and the sight of Kent's melting face elicits a "What the hell?!" from the janitor.

Kent takes a couple of steps toward the man, who backs out of the room, never taking his eyes off him. "Lemme explain," Kent says.

"Keep away from me!" the janitor commands.

"This is just a big misunderstanding." Kent removes his shirt, revealing his mushy and sagging body.

The man unhooks a walkie-talkie from a holster on his belt and presses a button. "Carl, get down to room—"

But before the janitor can finish his sentence, Kent's torso fans out like a cobra and swooshes down on the terrified man, completely enveloping him like plastic wrap over leftovers. His body muffles the man's screams as he struggles to break free. The janitor's hands bulge from beneath Kent's body, but he's unable to break through. My friend's face is stretched out, and his eyes are as big as dinner plates. The janitor's struggling finally subsides, and his muffled pleading for help softens, until he's still.

"You didn't kill him, did you?" I ask.

"I might look grotesque, but I ain't no monster," Kent says, unwrapping himself from around the man, who collapses to the floor, the flashlight and walkie-talkie dropping out of his hands. "Just choked the air outta him." His form returns to its original shape and he takes off down the hall, his flesh jiggling like a Jell-O Surprise.

Standing over the unconscious janitor, I see his chest move up and down. Relief washes over me that he's not seriously hurt.

"Marvin, come on," Kent yells.

I turn and chase after my friend, who's swallowed by the darkness at the end of the hall.

SEVENTEEN

The next evening, Eliza and I are in her car. She turns into a shopping mall parking garage. I hear people refer to this shopping center as Murder Mall. There have been a number of homicides here. One in particular was committed with a plastic fork from the food court. People's resourcefulness when it comes to evil never ceases to amaze me.

The mall has closed for the night. With the exception of a few abandoned vehicles, the garage is empty. We drive up the circular ramp to the top floor and come to a stop at the far side of the structure, which is the size of a football field. There is an open parking spot between some of the mall security and maintenance vehicles, and Eliza pulls her car into the space. She turns off the vehicle and looks at the dashboard clock. "They should be here any minute," she mumbles.

"Who?"

"Don't worry your pretty little head about it," Eliza says. "We're just backup, but if anything goes down, follow my lead."

"What's going to go down?" I ask.

I don't know if she didn't hear me or if she's just ignoring me, but she leans her head back and gazes up at the dark sky through the sunroof. "The only thing I miss from back home is being able to see the stars. On a crisp winter night, you can see all of the Milky Way."

"Are … are you from up … there?"

"Huh?"

I point up to space.

She rolls her eyes. "You've got to stop believing everything you read in the paper."

We sit in silence as we stare up through the sunroof.

"Hey, did Dr. Klaus get those results from my tests?" I ask.

"No, not—"

A roar at the other end of the parking structure interrupts her as three identical black street racers launch into the air off the lip of the ramp, landing on the top level. The vehicles skid to a stop. Three sets of blue headlights appear like sinister eyes looking for prey. From this distance, it's impossible to see who's behind the wheels of the cars. "Who are they?" I ask.

"Gamblers who just had their bluff called."

Something's not right. It takes me a second to put a finger on it, but when it occurs to me, it sends a shiver up my spine—fear. Eliza's fear bubbles to the surface. I can't imagine what would make a member of the Core afraid. And if she's afraid, then I should be terrified.

"… Eliza?"

"There he is," she says.

Sling approaches the vehicles. I don't know where he came from. He appeared out of nowhere. Sling is a member of the Core. His costume is an exaggerated version of a weightlifter's outfit, a one-piece leotard that hugs the contours of his bulging body. A little too tightly, if you ask me. It's the most ridiculous costume ever. The blue headlights wash over him as he faces down the three speedsters.

The driver's side door of the car nearest to Sling opens. A black biker boot plants firmly on the ground. A fat, balding man with a comb-over steps out of the car. He's the kind of guy who leaves greasy fingerprints on his drinking glass. While we can't hear what's being discussed, it's apparent by their body language that the man and Sling are arguing. Sling takes a step toward the man, who immediately pulls out a gun. He levels it at the member of the Core.

"Be cool," Eliza mutters. I don't know if she's saying it for my benefit or her own.

A woman wearing a skintight red racing suit and sporting a shaved head gets out of another car, and she aims some sort of weapon at Sling.

"This just went from bad to baby bad bitch," Eliza says.

Out of the corner of my eye, I see someone in the rearview mirror. Rocket is standing behind our vehicle, surveying the scene at the other end of the parking structure. As far as I know, Rocket's only power is that he can fly. And while his monochromatic brown costume might suggest that he's dull and drab, nothing could be further from the truth. I've seen some of his interviews, and I think he's the smartest member of the Core. He speaks like a professor—people grumble that they have to use a dictionary to even understand what he's saying. Over the last couple of years, he's cut back on giving interviews, and the rumor is that he refuses to dumb down what he says and would rather not saying anything at all.

Eliza rolls down her window as Rocket approaches. "I'm here if you need me," she says.

He doesn't say anything, just stands there watching the situation unfold, until he shoots into the air and disappears from sight. Then he swoops down and grabs the woman with the gun. Both disappear into the sky. The woman's weapon drops to the ground. A moment later, she crashes down on the hood of her car, denting the metal and shattering the windshield.

"What the hell?!" I say.

His gun never wavering from Sling, the balding man glances at the woman's motionless body. He glances toward the sky. Apparently spotting Rocket, he lifts his gun and fires it repeatedly into the air.

Taking the opportunity while the man's distracted, Sling runs toward him like a charging bull. Realizing he's about to get run over, the man aims the gun back at Sling, but it's too late. He's knocked off his feet and flies through the air, smacking the side of his car with the force of a wrecking ball. His unconscious body is wedged into the crumpled metal door.

The tires squeal on the remaining car, kicking up smoke as the driver attempts to get away.

"We're up," Eliza says, turning the key in the ignition. But the engine doesn't turn over. She tries again, but the car doesn't start. "Goddammit!"

The black car speeds off, heading toward the ramp.

Eliza tries the car again, but with the same sputtering result. "What're you waiting for?!" she yells. "Go after that car!"

She shoots up fear like a geyser. I drink it in, fueling myself.

I speed after the fleeing car. The high-pitched whir from

the engine winds up the circular ramp below me, like some deranged audible snake. Exiting the parking garage, I find myself on a one-way street, which takes the guesswork out of which way the vehicle went.

As I blur through an intersection, I glance left and see the black car, two blocks down. It's too late to change direction, so I keep going straight, but I take the first left I come to, which leads me through an alley that runs parallel to the surface street.

The alley runs into another street, but a street sweeper running a night route blocks me. I dig in and race toward the vehicle as fast as I can. Just before I'd slam into it, I leap up, propelling myself over the hulking machine. Sailing through the air, I scan the area, spotting the black car a block farther down. Landing on the other side of the street sweeper, I continue through the alley. Hitting the surface street, I take a hard left, then a right, gaining on the car ahead. I swerve in and out of traffic.

I come up beside the car, slowing down just enough to peer in through the window. Behind the wheel sits a young man with black racing clothes. Beads of sweat cover his brow like pimples. His eyes dart from the road to the rearview mirror and back again. My fingers slide under the door handle. He has one hand on the wheel and one resting on the stick shift. I yank the door open and reach inside, straining to reach across him. I take hold of the emergency brake and pull it. Right as the car's tires lock up, I rest the full weight of my body on the guy's lap, lifting my feet up as the car spins wildly out of control before skidding to a stop.

I rip open the guy's seat belt and hoist him out of the

car. He dangles above the ground. It takes a moment for him to realize what's just happened. "You can have it! Take it!" he yells, struggling to put something in my hand. "It's yours. I told them blackmail was a bad idea."

With one hand holding the guy up, his feet dangling over the ground, I open my other hand and look at the smiley-face sticker he gave me. It's about the size of a quarter.

"The data sticker. It's all in there. Take it. I don't want it. Don't worry 'bout the money," he says.

"Data sticker?" I ask.

"The video," he says. "It's yours. Let's just forget any of this happened, okay? I won't say a word. Promise."

"What video?"

Terror registers on the guy's face. "They're coming! Hurry! They're going to kill me!"

"Who is?"

He looks right at me and screams, "The Core!"

"The Core?" I say. "They're the good guys."

I hear a car come up behind us, rolling to a stop. The guy freaks out, trying desperately to tear away from my grasp. "Lemme go!" he cries.

A hand rests gently on my shoulder. It's Eliza. "You can set him down," she says.

I lower the guy to his feet and suddenly feel incredibly tired. "Roisin ..." And that's all I manage to croak before collapsing to the ground.

I don't know how long I'm out, but I wake up just as Eliza removes a needle from my leg. "You all right?" she asks.

The stuff works quickly. I get to my feet and say, "Was that the blue stuff?"

"Yep," she says.

We're in the middle of the street where I caught up with the car, but now the black speedster and its frightened driver are nowhere to be found. "Where's the car?"

"What car?"

"The car I chased down," I say.

She stares blankly at me.

I point to where he skidded to a stop. "The car was right there. See? The tire skid marks? The black street racer was right there. Where'd it go?"

"It was towed."

"How long was I out?" I ask.

She shrugs and says, "Oh, I don't know. About an hour I guess."

"Why didn't you inject me sooner?"

She walks toward her car. "There was no need to."

"What happened to the guy?"

"He was arrested." We get into her car and she starts it.

"What was that all about?" I ask.

"What do you mean?"

"The people at the parking garage?" I say. "What did they do?"

"That's classified." She puts the car in gear and steps on the gas.

"Did they die?" I ask. "The balding guy and the lady? Were they—"

"Marvin, you've got to stop asking so many questions."

"But—"

"Asking questions seriously puts in doubt your application to the Core," Eliza says.

After merging onto the freeway, we drive in silence for a while. "As a recruit, you're on a need-to-know basis, and you don't need to know," she adds.

I can't allow myself to think that I just witnessed the murder of those people, but there's no way a normie could survive a fall from that height or walk away from being slammed into that car. Maybe they were dirties. Perhaps they just got a little banged up but walked away unharmed. That's what I want to believe.

Desperately trying to think about something else, I wonder what happened to the smiley-face data sticker, because it was gone when I woke up.

EIGHTEEN

Eliza made plans to pick me up the following night. I was supposed to work at Midtown Café, but I called in sick. With Yvonne working there now, I figured Gus had enough staff to cover my waiter duties.

Eliza said it was important for me to get back in the saddle again. She didn't want me sitting around thinking about how things had gotten slightly out of control at the parking garage.

While it's not as famous as Mystic's Jet Car, Roisin's all-white ride takes a close second. The government-issued license plates read *Core #6*. When I get in, the vehicle reeks of roses, like an overzealous detailer sprayed too much air freshener inside. Eliza is wearing her Roisin costume. She fidgets with her white miniskirt, trying to pull it down where it's riding up on her thighs. If it was just an inch shorter, it would go from a PG-13 to an R. Her halter top reveals her bronzed and taut stomach, and her stiletto heels are so high she might as well be wearing stilts.

She notices me staring and smiles. "You should've seen what they wanted me to wear originally," she says. "Thank goodness my contract had a clause giving me costume approval."

"Do I get costume approval?"

She looks at me—or, more specifically, at my costume. I'd always envisioned myself in a cool costume, like a black leather biker jacket and matching boots. I wanted to wear something tough, something that would strike fear into the hearts of evildoers.

What she makes me wear is not that outfit.

I look like I work at one of those medieval-themed restaurants, where employees wear tunics and chain mail in an attempt to re-create eleventh-century life. This costume might actually be more ridiculous than Sling's weightlifting getup.

"You look cute," she says.

"I look like an idiot."

"People will remember you."

"That's what I'm afraid of."

She looks me up and down. "It'll do," she says, handing me a helmet. "Try this on."

The helmet is heavier than it looks. It's clunky and I can't see very well out of it. "This is so stupid. Where'd you get this?"

"It's a prototype costume," she says.

She shifts the car into gear and hits the accelerator. The car spins out and fishtails as we explode from zero to sixty almost instantly. Fumbling for the seat belt, I fasten it as we shoot out of the parking lot and onto the street, cutting off oncoming traffic. A cacophony of horns blares in unison as we speed away.

"Are we in a hurry?" I ask.

"Marvin, I'm always in a hurry," she says, weaving in and out of traffic.

We're halfway through the block when the light up ahead turns yellow. She presses the accelerator all the way to the floor. It turns red, and luckily she stomps on the brakes, squealing to a sudden stop at the intersection. I plant my hands on the dashboard to brace myself. A car horn makes Eliza look into the rearview mirror, raise her gloved hand, and flip the middle finger. "Don't you dare honk at me," she shouts. The light turns green, and she stomps on the gas pedal.

There's a ringing as a red light flashes on the dashboard. "Sorry, but I've got to take this call," she says, pressing a button on the steering wheel. "This is Roisin."

"Roisin, I'm going to need you to handle a 2-11 in progress near 46th and Pine," a man's voice says. There's a lot of distortion coming through the call, like the person on the other end is yelling into a phone while standing in a wind tunnel.

At the next light, Roisin takes a hard left. "I'm on my way," she says.

"I'd deal with it myself," the voice says, "but I've got to pay a visit to the Frontera Cartel."

Eliza glances at me. "You're on speaker, and I've got a civilian in the car."

The line goes silent.

"You should've said that out of the gate," the voice finally says.

"Marvin, do you wanna say hi?" she asks.

"Who is it?" I whisper.

"Mercury."

Stunned, I look at the speaker, realizing I'm listening to my hero—Lieutenant Mercury. I'm so overcome, I think I might have an anxiety attack.

Eliza nudges me with an elbow and says, "Say hi."

"Hi," I croak.

"Who's that?" Lieutenant Mercury asks.

"Marvin," Eliza says as she maneuvers through traffic. "He's a friend."

"Howdy, Marvin. I hope you can hear me. There tends to be a little distortion when I'm flying."

"You're flying right now?" I ask. "Like, not in a plane, right?"

Mercury chuckles. "No, not in a plane."

"He's up above it all," Eliza says.

"That is so cool," I say.

"Marvin, I've got to go, but it was nice chatting with you." The line goes dead.

"I just talked to Lieutenant Mercury! That's so freaking cool!"

"Hero worshipper," Eliza says, grinning.

"Whatever."

The car speeds toward a red light, and Eliza pushes down on the gas. I begin to scream when I realize she has no plan to stop. We bolt through the red light and miraculously make it through the traffic unharmed. "There's an armed robbery in progress," she says. "You ready to get into the mix?"

"Really?"

"It's time to step up to the plate," Eliza says. "You okay with that? If not, you can wait in the car."

"I'm ready."

I'm more nervous than I can ever remember being. This is it. This is what I've been dreaming about since I was a little kid. My chance to be a hero. A real hero. I pray that I don't screw up. I want to hit this out of the park.

Up ahead, the entire street is cordoned off with yellow police tape. It looks like the entire fleet of Loganstin police cruisers have formed a barrier around the block. A throng of spectators gathers on the other side of the barrier.

Eliza repeatedly honks her horn as she drives through the crowd. When the people realize it's Roisin who's trying to get through, they cheer wildly and swarm the car like locusts, slapping the vehicle and shouting encouragement to the youngest member of the Core. As people plaster their faces against the glass to sneak a peek inside, Eliza glances over at me and says, "It's a good thing I brought you that costume when I did. There was a clean, like, ten years ago who was a real hard-ass, and he decided to not wear a costume. He let it all hang out. Someone he pissed off tracked down the guy's uncle. That didn't end well."

"What happened?"

"His uncle was used to send a message, which they carved into the guy with razorblades." Eliza chuckles. "You only have your dad, right? And he's already in prison, and I'm guessing you probably don't really care if he's whacked. But better safe than sorry."

It feels like she punched a fist through my chest and squeezed my heart. Images of my mother flash through my head. While she's right about my father, I think of Yvonne and Kent. I flip down the helmet's visor.

Eliza manages to get through the crowd and approach the

police tape. Two young officers spot the car and hold the yellow tape up, allowing us to drive through. Eliza stops the car and gets out.

As soon as I open the door, I hear a barrage of bullets being fired. It sounds like we've just entered a war zone. Eliza's talking to Loganstin's chief of police, Earl Wooden, a weathered man with a deep and raspy voice that's probably due to years of smoking. It's well documented that he has an uneasy relationship with the Core. While still a homicide detective, he gave an interview in which he stated that the Core did little to assist the department with real police work. Wooden claimed the costumed heroes were only ceremonial crime fighters. He'd taken heat for comments like that, and many were shocked when he was appointed chief of police.

True to form, Wooden stares at Eliza with a thinly veiled look of irritation.

"What's the situation?" she asks.

Wooden doesn't attempt to conceal his disdain for the teenager dressed in white as he considers whether or not to enlist her help. I'm sure his ego doesn't like the idea of asking a young girl for assistance. But if Eliza sees this, she doesn't show it. Then Wooden looks me up and down and says, "Who's that?"

"A friend," she says.

"Is the Core recruiting at the Renaissance faire?" He chuckles.

"Are we going to make small talk or get down to business?" Eliza says.

Wooden bristles, apparently not accustomed to getting talked down to by a teenager. "Okay. An hour ago, two heavily armed assailants in body armor strolled into the Loganstin

First Bank and shot up the place. When they came out, my men were waiting," he says.

"Where are they now?"

Pointing down the street, the police chief says, "You can't hear the gunfire?"

The muzzle flashes from the gunfight around the corner cast an orange glow on the side of the building. There's a series of bursts of light, and it takes a few more seconds before I hear the sound produced by the gunshots. There's a stream of orange flares in rapid succession, which makes it look like an orange strobe light is pointed at the side of the building. The noise that follows is unmistakably that of automatic weapons.

Heading down the street, Eliza says, "Wooden, tell your men to stay out of our way. We'll handle this."

The chief of police curses under his breath. He glares at me as I hurry by him.

We peer around the corner of the building, and I'm unprepared for what I see. The entire scene seems to be ripped from a Modern Warfare video game. Two men dressed in head-to-toe body armor brandish automatic rifles. They have a variety of handguns in holsters on their belts. The men fire their weapons randomly across the street, hitting everything and anything. Fifteen members of the Loganstin SWAT team take cover behind squad cars and inside doorways. Two police cruisers are engulfed in flames. A wounded member of the SWAT team is pinned down behind one of the burning cars. The two gunmen riddle the car with bullets—it looks like a block of Swiss cheese on the verge of being blown to shreds. When the two men in body armor run out of bullets, the SWAT team emerges from behind their cover and fire their guns at them, but the bullets ricochet off the impenetrable suits of armor.

Eliza surveys the situation and recites her findings: "Two shooters wearing Aramid body armor with illegally modified assault rifles, including three Romanian AIM rifles, a modified HK-91, and an AR-15. A dozen or so SWAT team members on scene, with one, possibly two, injured and in between the crossfire."

"What do we do?" I ask, a lump in my throat.

Eliza steps out from behind the brick wall and stands in the middle of the road. Her eyes begin to glow bright red. The air around her begins to crackle, and it smells like ozone. The glowing intensifies, building up in force. Then a burst of red energy erupts from her eyes and shoots down the street. The assailant doesn't even see it coming as it hits him on the left side of his body and blows a hole through him, severing his body in two.

"Oh my god," I say. "You killed him."

It takes a moment for the other gunman to process what just happened to his partner. He stops firing and looks at his friend, who lies in two parts in a pool of blood and charred flesh. Following the direction of the blast, the man spots Eliza standing in the middle of the road. Her eyes begin to glow again, building up strength for another blast. Realizing the dire situation he's in, the man runs toward the burning squad car and the wounded SWAT team member, who fires his gun at him. As the bullets clank off the assailant's armor, he rips the rifle out of the wounded man's hands, grabs him, and hoists him to his feet. He uses the grimacing SWAT team member as a shield from Eliza.

"Marvin, you're up," Eliza says. The glowing red energy in her eyes dims.

"What?"

"I don't have the best aim," she says. "Do your thing."

"What do you want me to do?" I ask.

"Use your power to end this," she says.

I stare at the severed corpse. I try to make sense of it. Just moments ago the guy was alive, and now he's dead, mowed down like a weed. And Eliza did it. She didn't even hesitate. It wasn't even a last resort. It was her first move. But the thing that troubles me the most is that it doesn't appear to affect her in the slightest. Just another day at the office.

"Marvin, any time now," Eliza snaps.

"I'm not going to kill him."

Backing away from the threat of Eliza, the gunman struggles to get his hostage to move. The SWAT team member is weak and stumbles to the ground. The rest of the SWAT team fires at the gunman, but the bullets just bounce off his body armor. Picking his hostage back up, the assailant continues to back away.

"Do something!" Eliza barks.

"Okay, okay," I say. I focus my energy on probing for fear. I try Eliza first, but she's not afraid. My feardar expands its search and reaches the wounded SWAT team member. Surprisingly, he isn't full of fear. But I hit pay dirt with his captor. The man in body armor must be sweating bullets. He has a reservoir of fear, like cool, dark waters held behind a massive dam. I tap into his fear and drink deeply.

"Marvin, if you don't—" Eliza starts to say, but I don't hear her finish because I'm already on the move.

I dash down the street, passing the assailant and his hostage. I circle around the two men three times while I consider my options. On the fourth pass, I pull back my arm and throw a punch at the side of the gunman's head. My fist connects with his metal helmet, and I feel it cave under the impact. Running around him three more times, I continue to hit him until he finally stumbles and collapses to the ground. The SWAT team member staggers on his feet before falling to the concrete.

I rip the weapons away from the gunman, tossing them across the street. He moans and tries to get to his feet. I pummel him with another series of blows. He gasps and falls back to the ground. This time he doesn't stir. I rest a hand on his chest and feel his heart beating.

Eliza waves over the SWAT team, saying, "You can come out now."

They hurry over and attend to their wounded team member. All of them shoot me looks, but no one says a word.

Nudging Eliza, I say, "Let's go."

"Are you crazy? The reporters will be here soon," she says. "We've got to do our interviews."

"No way. Not me."

"That's the best part of our job," she says. "If you don't get it on camera, it might as well not have happened."

Leaning in close to her ear, I whisper, "I'm going to crash."

"Remind me to snag some of Dr. Klaus's go-go juice. I can't always worry about you passing out on me."

I take one last look at the corpse. Steam is rising off the charred flesh.

Itching to get as far away from there as possible, I speed off down the street, passing a swarm of television reporters breaking down their cameras from where they were positioned, apparently documenting the whole event. As I race home, passing vehicles in a blur, I hope nobody will be able to identify me tonight—and by nobody, I mean Yvonne.

NINETEEN

I remove my costume and stuff it into a discarded plastic grocery bag before stepping into the concrete cave. Yvonne's curled up on the sofa, a blanket draped over her. There's an empty to-go container from Midtown Café and the gnawed-on remains of BBQ ribs. A late-night sketch comedy show runs on the television. She looks so peaceful and content while she sleeps. I pull the blanket up around her shoulders, tucking the corners around her. Picking up the remote, I turn off the television. I want to wake Yvonne up and tell her about what happened tonight. I want to tell her about Eliza. I want to tell her everything.

But I don't. Instead, I walk away.

Passing Kent's room on the way to mine, I see he's slouched over his desk, working on a new plaster mold. He's using a tiny brush to sweep away imperfections.

"Knock knock," I say.

"Where've you been?"

"Out."

"Dude, you don't look so good," Kent says.

I don't have much more left in my tanks. I imagine that I probably look as bad as I feel. "Yeah."

His nostrils flare and he sniffs the air. "Do you smell that?" he asks.

"What?"

"It smells like burnt meat."

A shiver runs through my body, and I don't know if it's because of the image of the charred corpse or how Eliza went from zero to kill in the blink of an eye.

"Kent, what's the worst thing you've ever witnessed?"

He looks up from his work and gives me a look. "Is this about that girl at the sandwich shop?"

"Huh?"

"What's on your mind?" he asks.

"Oh, it's nothing," I say. "I'm going to bed."

"Marvin, is this about Roisin?" His face doesn't register anger, mistrust, or judgment. It registers concern. Concern for a friend.

"Forget it," I say, heading to my room. "Good night."

The next morning, I wake up from my coma-like sleep and step out of my room with nothing on my mind except eating. On the way to the kitchen, I glance into the living room and don't see my friends. I might be able to convince them I was just sleepy and that's why I slept so long. But if they catch me shoveling food into my mouth, they'll know I used my powers and there'll be endless questions.

I find a bag of chocolate cookies, cram them into my mouth, and head outside. On the way to the Gas 'n' Sip, I think about last night and, again, how Eliza acted. Perhaps that's what's required of members of the Core—just act, don't think. I know that I overanalyze everything. I spend so much time thinking about how I should act, I tend to not do anything. In life-and-death situations, heroes must act. You never hear stories about soldiers who freeze and do nothing. Soldiers who spring into action are the ones we celebrate and award medals to. Eliza is a soldier who acts.

Not many customers use baskets in a convenience store, but not everybody is starving after a night of corralling bank robbers with a member of the Core. Grabbing the one and only basket, I walk up and down the aisles, loading up on whatever looks good and some things that don't. A little bit of this, a couple more of those, and a whole lot of that.

As I'm piling discounted canned food into the basket, I notice the magazine rack. The morning papers feature out-of-focus photos of me decked out in the tunic and helmet. I pick up the *Loganstin Journal* and look at the photo. The headline reads, *The Core's Newest Recruit?* I skim the article and see that Roisin was quoted answering a question about me, remarking, *"He's a friend."*

"Is he clean?"

"Of course he's clean."

That's news to me.

As I scan the paper, something else becomes apparent—there's no photo or mention of the dead assailant. The focus of this story seems to be the guy I knocked unconscious. There are even photos of him being led away in handcuffs.

All those reporters, photographers, and camera crews were right there. On the spot. They *must* have documented Eliza taking the guy out. I get the decision to not publish photos of the crispy critter, but burying the fact that there were two culprits boggles my mind. How can they keep that quiet and under wraps? There were too many witnesses.

The cashier rings up my items. As I dig into my pocket for money, he bags my purchases, pausing to look at the blurry photo on the cover of one of the newspapers. "Man, I wish I had the original papers that first ran stories about Lieutenant Mercury," he says. "Do you know how much they go for now?"

"No."

"The first edition of the *Loganstin Journal* issue is worth ten thousand dollars."

"Wow," I say, handing over my money and motioning to the newspapers. "Well, they're running stories about a new guy. Maybe you should pick up a couple of copies."

The cashier puts the money in the register. "Ain't no way someone looking that stupid is gonna command top dollar," he says.

I've consumed nearly half a bag of goodies by the time I get home. As I walk toward the living room, I see the television casting a flickering light on the outside wall. I step into the room and plop down in a chair. Yvonne and Kent are sitting on the sofa. I open another bag of snacks and say, "Do you guys want something?"

"You got any donuts in there?" Kent asks. Retrieving a package of donuts, I toss them to him. "Thanks, homie," he says.

"Yvonne?"

"The only thing I want is an explanation," she says, turning up the volume on the television. It's a special report, and the footage shows the robbery last night. More specifically, me pummeling the gunman.

Yvonne's eyes remain fixed on the television. Her jaw muscles are clenched. Kent shoves a small donut into his gaping maw and glances at her, then at me. His eyes continue to dart back and forth like a spectator at a tennis match, waiting to see who's going to go first.

"Do you have anything to say?" Yvonne asks.

"About what?"

She motions to the television. "About that." A close-up of me wearing that ridiculous helmet is superimposed on the screen.

"Why do you think that's me?" I say.

Yvonne reaches behind the sofa and retrieves the helmet. She tosses it across the room at me. It hits my chest and clanks to the floor.

"You rummaged around my room?"

"Marvin, don't. Just don't," she says.

"Roisin tracked him down at Midtown after he saved the family," Kent says.

Yvonne turns her glare on Kent. "You knew about this?"

Kent grimaces, recognizing that he just stumbled into a trap. "Um…yeah. I guess."

"Why'd she want to track you down?" Yvonne asks, turning her icy stare to me.

"To talk," I say.

"To talk?"

"Yeah."

"About what?"

"Stuff," I say. "You know."

"So, the two of you talk, and then you're fighting crime. Is that about right?" Yvonne asks.

"Yeah, I guess."

She laughs, a humorless laugh. "Fighting crime. The Core fighting crime. That's rich."

"Yvonne, what's your deal?" I ask. "What's your problem with the Core?"

"What's my problem? The Core is worse than any of the criminals they've ever put behind bars," she snaps.

I say, "You don't know what you're talking about."

Yvonne rustles in the sofa, but her eyes never shift away from the television. "Lieutenant Mercury killed my parents."

The only sound I hear comes from the television, and it suddenly sounds like it's blaring. Kent picks up the remote and turns it off. But Yvonne's eyes remain fixed on the blank screen. "I was getting ready for school. My mom laid out clothes for me to wear. My dad had just gotten home from working a graveyard shift, but he took time to make me breakfast. My parents spent the last few moments of their lives taking care of me. Before I even made it to the sidewalk, something fell out of the sky and crashed into our home."

Yvonne tells how she ran back inside. Her parents were buried under rubble. They were dead. But Mercury got to his feet and staggered out the door like he was drunk and leaving a party. Yvonne watched, tears running down her face, as the leader of the Core leaped into the sky and flew away, disappearing into the clouds.

"A handful of black SUVs skidded to a stop on the street," she says. "Men in suits and sunglasses got out. They told me that it was a horrible tragedy. They told me to go with them and they'd figure it out. But they already had it figured out. I got a hundred dollars and was dropped off at child services. A hundred dollars? Like that would cover the cost of my pain."

"Oh my god," Kent says. "What happened?"

"I'll tell you exactly what happened," she says. "The bastards went to work and ruined the reputations of my mom and dad. They claimed my parents were violent suspects with a long history of criminal activities. This version of events was dutifully repeated again and again by the local media." She turns to me, and I swear I can feel the anger radiating off her body. "Do you know why my parents were killed? There was no reason for it. None. Mercury fucked up, and his fuck-up killed my parents."

"Yvonne," I say, "are you—"

"You know what the real pisser is? Them trying to cover up the mistake by making my mom and dad out to be monsters. They weren't monsters. They were just parents trying to protect their daughter—but they couldn't protect me from the Core. Nobody is protected from them."

"That's messed up," Kent says.

"I hate the Core. I hate everything they represent," Yvonne says. "If I could, I'd burn them all to the ground."

"But it's not like that," I say. "I mean—"

Yvonne gets up. She opens her mouth to say something but stops herself. Then she says, "You need to move out."

"What?"

"I think it's for the best."

"Yvonne, come on," Kent says.

She hurries out of the room.

Kent and I are both stunned. Neither one of us says anything, because at this point there's nothing really to say. The silence just seems to stretch on.

Finally, Kent motions to the cookies. "Can I have one?"

I hold out the bag and he takes one, tossing it into his mouth whole. I look at him, shrug, and say, "I guess I'll go pack my things."

"Give her some time," he says. "She'll get over it."

I stuff my handful of T-shirts, socks, underwear, and jeans into a duffel bag. It dawns on me that relationships that were years in the making can be destroyed, and you won't even know it until it's already happened. As I step out into the hall, I see a light glowing from Yvonne's room. I consider trying to talk to her, but then reconsider. I sling my duffel bag over my shoulder and head out.

TWENTY

Eliza steers her orange car down a maze of deserted streets in Bixby Gardens, heading toward the rundown building where her safe house is hidden. She drives around back and parks.

"Are you sure this is okay?" I ask. "I didn't know where else to go."

"Of course," she says. "I'm hardly ever here anyway. *Mi casa es su casa.*"

Once inside the apartment, she heads into the kitchen and opens the stainless steel refrigerator, pulling out a carton of milk. "You want something to drink?" she asks.

"Nah."

"Come on. We're celebrating your new life."

"Um … okay," I say. "Just one."

She grabs two glasses from the cabinet and pours them half full of milk, then sets the carton down and produces a brown bottle of liquor from underneath the counter. She pours the booze into both glasses, filling them to the brim, and slides a glass to me. I pick it up and look at the cloudy cocktail.

"What? You don't like Kahlua and milk?" she asks. "This is a girlie drink, so you'll probably like it."

I take a sip, trying to be gracious. It doesn't taste half bad, kind of like chocolate milk with a kick. I pretend to take another drink and set the glass down. Eliza tilts her head back and drains the entire glass. She wipes the milk mustache from her upper lip and pours herself another one. "Why aren't you drinking?"

"I've got a shift tonight at Midtown Café," I say.

"You haven't quit yet?"

"No. I just called in sick yesterday."

"You've got to quit. You can't have a job while trying out for the Core." She hands me the phone.

"But I have a shift tonight."

"What did I just say?"

"But what am I going to do about money?" I ask.

"Once you're a member of the Core, you'll have everything you need."

"But I can't just—"

She slams her glass down hard on the counter and glares at me. Her eyes are already glassy and slightly unfocused. "You want a moment?"

The phone feels heavy in my hands. I nod my head yes.

Eliza carries her drink and wobbles out of the kitchen. I dial the number. The phone on the other end is picked up and I hear a woman's voice say, "Midtown Café. How may I help you?"

"Phyllis?" I say.

"Yeah. Who's this?"

"Marvin."

"What's up?"

"Is Gus there?"

"Hold on," Phyllis says.

The line is muted as the call is transferred. Before I can even rehearse what I'm going to say, I hear Gus's voice. "Marvin, please tell me you're not calling in sick again. It's busy, and we're swamped."

"Um, Gus…"

There's a pause as Gus waits for me to continue, but when I don't, he asks, "Is everything okay?"

"I'm not going to be able to come in tonight."

"Marvin, what's wrong?"

"Nothing."

"Are you in trouble?"

"No."

"Tell me what's going on."

I don't know if it's my guilt or Gus sounding so concerned, but I snap, "Gus, I'm quitting! Got it? I can't work for you anymore."

"Why not?"

"I've got other things going on right now," I say.

"What kinda things?"

"Things."

Gus clears his throat and says, "Marvin, I'm disappointed in you. I thought we were friends, but friends don't treat each other like this."

"Gus—"

"Bring your key back," he says.

"Come on, Gus," I say. "It's not like—"

The line goes dead as Gus hangs up the phone.

That phone conversation went as badly as I'd initially feared. Worse, actually. Sometimes my worst fears are realized, which is an occurrence that seems to be happening with more frequency lately.

"Marvin, c'mere!" Eliza calls from the bedroom, her voice heavy and lazy from the effects of the alcohol.

As I step into the room, she grabs me and kisses me forcefully on the mouth. I taste the sourness of the alcohol. She pushes me onto the bed, climbs on top of me, and begins to take off my clothing.

"No," I say. She pulls my T-shirt over my head. "Eliza, stop it."

She slaps me hard across the face. "Nobody tells me what to do," she yells.

"Get off!"

She shoves me hard, back onto the mattress. Her eyes begin to glow and she fixes her deadly stare right at my head. "Tell me what to do again. I dare you."

I don't move a muscle. I don't even breathe. The heat from her radiating eyes washes over me. Slowly and meticulously, she unbuttons her blouse. She continues to undress, never taking her eyes off me. She leans down and kisses my neck. The energy from her eyes scalds my skin. On my back, I stare up at the ceiling, taking great pains not to look at her as she takes control.

Out of breath and heaving, Eliza collapses on top of me. She lies there for a moment, and when she pushes herself up, her eyes are no longer glowing. Brushing her hair out of her eyes, she puts her clothes on. Without even so much as a backward glance, she staggers out of the room, leaving me on the bed. The keys rattle as she grabs them, followed by the slamming of the front door.

By the time I get up and look out the window, she's driving away, disappearing into the night. Catching her scent, I wince in disgust. I don't even find the light fragrance of roses pleasant anymore.

Entering the bathroom, I turn on the shower and let the water heat up. The steam fogs the mirror, which is good, because it prevents me from seeing my reflection. I'm sure I wouldn't like what I'd see in there.

TWENTY-ONE

I wake up with the warm sunshine beating against the outside of the safe-house blinds. There's an empty pit where my stomach is, and I try to remember when I last ate. I get out of bed, put my clothes on, and walk into the kitchen. There's no sign of Eliza. I open the refrigerator and find condiments—ketchup, mayonnaise, mustard—a half-empty plastic bottle of water, and an assortment of beer. Not much in the way of food. Opening a large kitchen cabinet, I find boxes of macaroni and cheese, noodles, and saltine crackers. I grab the crackers and rip open the box. I plop down on the sofa, turn on the television, and eat.

Four hours later, the crackers are gone and I've lost interest in the television. I wonder when Eliza is coming back. I pick up the phone and dial her number. The phone rings and rings. I keep expecting it to go to voicemail, but it doesn't. I let it ring thirty times before I finally give up.

I'm furious. Nothing is how I expected it to be. My mind races in a thousand different directions at the same time. I've got to get out of this apartment.

As I walk through Bixby Gardens, the abandoned buildings project fingerlike shadows onto the empty streets. A rusted and eroded sign hangs whopper-jawed from the front of a ten-story warehouse. It reads *Cache Valley Manufacturing*, and I'm surprised to realize that I've heard of this place. Decades ago, it was a goliath of American industry at its best. The chain-link fence around the perimeter of the building has toppled, in no position to keep anything out. I step over the fence and head toward the front of the building.

Large panes of glass in the revolving door are shattered, so I hunker over and step inside. The marble floors in the expansive lobby are stained and damaged. Three support pillars rise from the foundation to the high ceiling. The middle pillar is cracked. I pick up a chunk of concrete and toss it at the damaged pillar. The impact dislodges a large section, which cascades to the floor with a rumble.

Something stirs within me. I find something satisfying about being responsible for this destruction. I'm powerless over the state of affairs in my life, but here I stand, instilling change upon my surroundings. Bending over, I gather pieces of lumber, clumps of rocks, and sections of pipe. One after the other, I throw them at the damaged pillar. Some miss completely but others slam into the growing cracks, which expand like tributaries in a flood.

I keep heaving heavier and heavier objects at the pillar. Anger boils with each item I toss. I hear a scream. It's my own voice, cheering me on as I destroy the pillar. I'm consumed with animal rage, incapable of harboring a clear thought. The pillar finally collapses onto the marble floor in a heap. I'm out of breath and sweating. The two adjacent pillars shift under the increased weight, bursting like matchsticks and bringing down the lobby ceiling.

I dash toward the revolving door as the ceiling topples down behind me. Dust and debris follow me out. Running a safe distance away, I turn around and marvel at the destruction caused by my own hand.

The plumes of dust and residue settle. A light breeze rustles my hair as I stand there, rooted in place. My anger is subsiding, replaced with a hollow sadness. I make my way back to the safe house, listening to the desolate wind blowing through the arid urban landscape.

The staircase groans under my weight as I make my way up to Eliza's apartment. I open the door and listen, but no sound greets me. At this point, I don't know if this disappoints me or not. My stomach growls. I don't think I possess the motivation to actually boil water to cook, so I grab a package of ramen, rip open the wrapping, and bite into the dry noodles, chewing them loudly.

Carrying a handful of the rock-hard pasta, I stop outside the door to Roisin's shrine and stare at her walls of memorabilia.

My gaze settles on the closet door and the security keypad. The tiny light is red. Just a few days ago, I never would've thought of going against something Eliza said, but too much has happened recently, and I find myself caring less and less. So I press the number 6 three times on the keypad, remembering how Eliza used this code to lock it.

The heavy lock slides open, and the light flashes green. I open the door. Darkness and a mechanical hum lie beyond the threshold. The closet space is deceptively big. It's filled with shelves lined with row after row of DVDs, memory cards, and jump drives. Two external hard drives hum and chirp as data is exchanged with a computer on a desk.

I pick up a glossy printout of what looks like a frame-grab from a video. And while the image is grainy and blurry, I know exactly what it is—it's an image of Eliza and me tangled together as one at the dam. High above the water suspended on top of the mist, Eliza and I suck face.

"Oh my god," I mutter. There was a camera there. From the angle of the image, it looks like it must've been near her car.

There's a device that plugs into the computer that looks like a thumbprint scanner. But on the pad is a smiley-face sticker. It looks like the data sticker the man tried to give me the other night. I jostle the mouse until the computer screen comes to life. An icon of a smiley-face appears on the computer's desktop, which I click on. It opens a media player.

The video begins to play, and it's clear the footage is from a security camera. The timestamp at the bottom of the screen states it was filmed a little over two years ago. I can see long tables in a room where men and women garbed in gloves, rubber aprons, and surgical masks scoop up large piles of white powder with mini garden shovels and deposit the substance into cellophane bags. There are guards with automatic rifles carefully watching the workers. Then three men enter the room. One is wearing an all-white suit. He inspects the workers like a CEO walking the assembly line in a factory.

A blinding light explodes and distorts the video's image. When it finally reappears, chaos has erupted. The workers have abandoned their posts and are running for cover. The guards fire their rifles at something off-screen. This seems to go on forever. Then, without warning, a bolt of energy strikes a guard and blows his head off. His body collapses to the ground. The beam fires again and hits another guard in the chest, blowing a nearly perfect hole through his body. A guard fires his gun and an instant later looks down, confused, at his empty hands, his rifle suddenly missing. A man appears out of nowhere and shoots a guard at point-blank range with the automatic weapon. Before the guard collapses to the floor, the shooter is gone.

In a matter of seconds, the guards are dead. As the dust settles, Eliza strolls into the room. She holds a leash that's attached to a collar fastened around the neck of a large lizard who is walking upright—McKay. She yanks on the leash, and McKay stumbles behind her. His wrists are bound together with zip ties and his face is covered in what I assume is blue blood.

A blur comes to a stop in front of Eliza. And though I've never seen his face unmasked, I know it's Streak. He's missing his front two teeth, and this strikes me as strange. But other than that, the man who is Streak is rather unremarkable-looking. He rounds up some of the cowering workers at gunpoint and motions for them to get back to work. They hesitate for only a moment and then turn and continue to bag up the white powder.

The video goes on for a while as the workers continue to fill the cellophane bags. Once they're done, Streak has them pick up the bundles and march off-screen. Eliza fastens the end of the leash to a table. McKay struggles, but it's pointless. Eliza walks off-screen, following Streak.

The video flicks and goes black.

So this is what really happened in Belize.

And the guy mentioned blackmail. This is what he was talking about. They were using this footage to blackmail the Core. It all makes sense now.

I click on other icons in the data sticker folder. Photo after photo show corpses lying in rubble, missing limbs, buildings demolished, and wreckages of airplanes. Whole city blocks are destroyed—concrete is torn back and pushed up into clumps, like a sheet kicked to the foot of a bed. Damaged cars and trucks are scattered about, and innocent bystanders try to dig people out of the wreckage. Corpses are shown twisted in unnatural positions. One collection of photos documents the collapse of a building.

The common theme, throughout these varied images of carnage and destruction, is Lieutenant Mercury.

I come across a series of photos that show him fighting Monger, and the total destruction of the Grinde Investment Building that was the result. So it wasn't two dirties fighting each other that destroyed the building in the business district, as was reported. Mercury was involved, not Gunner.

"Mercury did all this?" I mutter, feeling like I've just woken up to a dark and grisly reality. I suddenly feel horrible for doubting Yvonne's story. Everything she told me about Mercury destroying her house and killing her parents, and the subsequent cover-up, was probably true. And I didn't believe her.

I didn't want to believe her.

I close out of the data sticker folder. Another icon on the desktop catches my attention—one with the file name *Marvin*. I double-click on it.

The media player opens and plays footage from last night—when Eliza forced herself on me. I'm dazed as I watch it, listening to my muffled voice telling her to leave me alone. But once her eyes radiate energy, I fall silent and lie motionless as a corpse. The camera films the entire event. And at one point, Eliza turns to the camera and smiles directly at it.

I leave the closet, head down the hall, and look around the bedroom. It doesn't take me too long to spot the tiny lens mounted on top of the mirror.

I suddenly feel ill.

Hurrying back to the closet, I'm just in time to see the footage that shows Eliza getting dressed and leaving me lying on the bed.

"Marvin, where are you?" Eliza calls from down the hall.

I close all the open windows on the computer.

Her footsteps echo on the hard floor.

Darting out of the closet, I shut the door.

She makes her way down the hallway toward the room. "Marvin?"

The light on the keypad is green. I type in the code and hit the *lock* button. The alarm chirps and turns red.

She pops her head in the doorway. I'm standing at a glass case staring at the various Roisin action figures. The smile on her face quickly disappears. "What do you think you're doing?" she asks.

"Nothing," I say.

"I was calling you."

"Oh, you were? I didn't hear you."

She stares at me for moment, then glances at the closet door. It could be my imagination, but she studies it longer than I would think necessary. "Come on," she says. "We've got an errand to run."

With that, she walks back out of the room. I breathe a sigh of relief as I follow her.

TWENTY-TWO

When I catch up to her downstairs, she's getting into her car. I buckle my seat belt as she checks her makeup in the rearview mirror before putting the car in gear and driving away. The silence between us is thick and uncomfortable, like oppressive humidity that you can't escape.

The drive takes forever. I look at her out of the corner of my eye and fantasize about confronting her about everything I know. I envision her getting tongue-tied and stammering over her words as she feebly attempts to counter the charges. But I don't, because whatever I do next, I don't want her to see it coming. I just need to come up with a plan fast. It feels like time is running out.

The car pulls up to a rundown Chinese restaurant and Eliza double-parks out front. "Okay, let's go."

As we get out of the vehicle, traffic builds up behind us. A couple of angry drivers honk their horns. "Are you going to move your car?" I ask.

"No time." She breezes past the front door of the restaurant, passing through a parade of men and women on the sidewalk. Stopping at the mouth of the alley adjacent to the restaurant, she motions me to her. Draping an arm around my shoulder, she leans in and says, "This is just in case."

A sharp pain explodes in my thigh. She's jammed three needles through my jeans and is squeezing the contents of three vials of Dr. Klaus's concoction into my leg.

"What the hell?" I scream.

Pulling out the needles, she winks at me and says, "Don't be such a sissy."

I rub my thigh. It stings. "Three vials? Am I gonna OD?"

"We've got to go," she says, heading into the alley. The sun, sinking into the horizon, casts the passage in shadows. The garbage dumpsters give off a musty odor. The soles of my shoes stick to the ground from the ooze produced from discarded Chinese food. Eliza leads me farther down the alley. "Just up here."

There's a clatter as garbage cans topple over. Eliza goes rigid as the silhouette of a man approaches us. As he gets closer, I can see he's wearing a suit, and a tie that's loosened around his neck. The jacket is draped over his shoulder, the collar hooked over his thumb. He's tall and muscular and strolls toward us like he doesn't have a worry in the world. His face is chiseled and he has piercing blue eyes.

Eliza looks around, searching for something. She puts an arm across my chest, like a driver who slams on the brakes and instinctively tries to hold back the passenger. "Marvin, stand right here," she says.

"Roisin, what's going on?" the man asks.

Eliza doesn't take her eyes off him. She's marinating in fear.

"Roisin?" I say.

The man in the suit looks at me. "Who's he?"

"He's my partner," she says.

He tosses his jacket on top of a nearby dumpster. "Well, kid, I'm sorry to hear that."

The man charges me. And by charge, I mean charges like a rhino. I reach out with my mind to feed off Eliza's fear. I just barely have time, but manage to power up a millisecond before the man bulldozes into me, sending me into a stack of wooden crates.

I jump up but the man's on me, firing a series of punches to my head and body. He grimaces. "You've got powers," he says. "Guess I don't have to pull my punches." He cocks his arm and throws another swing, which sinks into my stomach. This one sends me flying back twenty feet, into a brick wall. I fall to the ground and my head slams down on the concrete.

Eliza shoots the man with a blast from her eyes. This only seems to irritate our attacker. He grabs her and hoists her into the air with one arm, as easily as if Eliza weighed no more than a baby. He slaps her across the face. "I've wanted to do that since I first met you!" he says. Then he heaves her through the air. Eliza lands on her stomach and skids to a stop deeper in the alley.

When his back is to me, I barrel into him with all the speed at my command. The impact launches the guy off his feet, sending him straight into the air. Shock and pain register on his face. He shoots up forty feet, but as he reaches the apex of the ascent, instead of crashing back to the ground, he hovers there. Overhead, he collects his bearings, shaking his head to clear the cobwebs.

He's a flier.

Then, screaming with the fury of an erupting volcano, he aims his feet at me, dropping from the sky like a bomb. I jump out of the way and his feet miss my head by an inch. His loafers smash into the concrete, cracking it open and leaving a crater. He turns and flies at me with his clenched fists outstretched like a battering ram. I'm fast, but not nearly fast enough. His fist clips me in the shoulder, spinning me around and around like a top. By the time I steady myself, he's picked me up over his head like a pro wrestler and tossed me against the brick wall. Dozens of bricks dislodge and crumble to the ground.

Lying on the ground in a heap, I cover my head with my arms as he kicks me repeatedly. "Who are you?" he yells. Pulling back his foot like a place kicker, he aims straight for my head. I grab his foot and yank him to the ground. Not letting go of his foot, I get up and lift him into the air. Like I'm cracking a whip, I hit him against the wall, then the ground, and into the other wall. Using both hands, I fling him out of the alley and into the dark storefront across the street. He crashes through the large glass window, toppling mannequins like bowling pins.

Eliza is battered and bruised, and her lip is split and bleeding. "Let's go!" I say, running farther down the alley.

She shuffles behind me, until finally she stops and steadies herself against a stack of wooden crates. "I can't …" she mumbles.

A breeze picks up, rustling debris and garbage. It's followed by what sounds like the air being cut overhead. I shove Eliza into a doorway, taking cover under the awning. The man flies above us, canvassing the area.

"Who is that guy?" I whisper.

She touches her lip with trembling fingers, pulling them away and seeing blood. "Darren Campbell," she says.

"Who's he?" I ask. "And what did you do to get him so mad?"

Eliza starts to reply, but goes silent when Darren stops in midair directly overhead. He searches for us and then moves on.

"Let's go," I say. We race down the alley, passing boarded-up windows and doors. As we bolt toward a busy street, a gust of wind rises up and washes over us. Darren is a bird of prey, flying overhead, tracking our every move. "Hurry!" I shout.

The flier circles around and heads right at us, diving out of the sky. "You've got to stop him!" Eliza shouts.

Darren swoops down with his fingers outstretched like talons, aiming right at Eliza. She screams.

It would be easy for me to slip away, leaving Eliza behind to deal with this lunatic. Heaven knows she doesn't deserve any better. But despite what she's done or the threats she's made, I can't. I just can't.

As he flies inches over my head, I reach up and grab him and, using all my strength, redirect his momentum into the ground, which he hits headfirst. The thud caused from the impact is deep, like an underground explosion. His head lies in an unnatural position on his still body.

Eliza takes a hesitant step toward the unconscious man. His chest slowly rises and falls. "He's still alive," she mutters.

"Come on!" I say, heading out of the alley. "Before he gets up."

She walks around the body lying amidst the scattered trash,

giving Darren a wide berth. His eyes are open, staring blankly toward the sky.

We duck out of the alley and merge with the pedestrian foot traffic. We get a couple of quizzical looks until we stop running and slow to a brisk walk. "What was that all about?" I drill her.

"We should go back and finish him off," she says. "He should be put down like an animal."

"I'm no killer, not like you."

Eliza storms ahead of me. "Wait for me back at the safe house."

Before I can say anything, she turns down another street and is gone.

TWENTY-THREE

I toss and turn all night, unable to fall asleep even though I'm exhausted. I finally drift off and don't wake up until the next afternoon. When I try Eliza's number, I actually get an answer this time. But it's an automated voice saying, "The number you have dialed has been disconnected. Please check the number and try again."

I hang the phone up and redial the number—but I get the same message.

Angry beyond belief, I plop down on the sofa. I flip channels, stopping when a program is interrupted by breaking news. An anchorwoman sits behind a desk. A photo of Lieutenant Mercury, in his yellow-and-black costume, is superimposed on the screen behind her. It says *R.I.P.* below him.

The anchorwoman says, "Our city's beloved hero and protector, Lieutenant Mercury, has been murdered. His body was found early this morning behind a restaurant on the thirty-six-hundred block of Hermosa Street."

My heart stops.

"The beloved hero's real name was Darren Campbell," the anchorwoman says.

And with those eight words, my whole life is leveled.

They flash a couple of photos of Darren not wearing his famous costume, and my worst fear is confirmed—it is without a doubt the same man who attacked Eliza and me.

The newscast then shows stock footage of soldiers storming an opulent desert palace. The anchorwoman's voice says, "A young Darren Campbell led Vector Squadron 3 to depose of the dictator Anas Sayed." An artist's depiction, much like a drawing in a comic book, shows Darren crushing an enemy tank with his bare hands. Soldiers jump out of the tank, fleeing for their lives.

"Darren's service during the Sidewinder mission is still classified to this day," the anchorwoman says. "But he's credited with turning the tide of the military campaign."

I fear a picture of my face will flash across the screen next, proclaiming me the murderer of this celebrated man. Of everyone's hero.

"There wasn't much information about Darren Campbell immediately after his military service," the anchorwoman says. "But in 1991, Darren revealed himself to the world as Lieutenant Mercury."

The newscast shows a series of photos of a masked Lieutenant Mercury performing acts of heroism. In a grainy photo, he swoops out of the sky to save a child trapped in a burning building. There are photos showing him fighting terrorists, both domestic and foreign, and various dirties whose names and abilities have long been forgotten.

"Lieutenant Mercury's crowning achievement came in

2001 when he decided to recruit worthy cleans to form the group known as the Core," the anchorwoman says. "This group has protected the citizens of Loganstin ever since."

The newscast shows Mystic, sitting in a chair and dabbing her eyes with a tissue. "This is a tragic day for all of humankind," Mystic says. "And I want to assure the world that the Core will not rest until Lieutenant Mercury's killer is brought to justice."

The anchorwoman says, "There is a memorial service planned for tonight at the Civic Center, downtown. The Core will be there to pay tribute to their fallen leader."

Turning off the television, I jump up, grab my jacket, and rush out the door. At least I know where I can find Eliza.

TWENTY-FOUR

The crowd grows steadily, and the flow of foot traffic becomes one large mass moving toward a common destination. Traffic is shut down to accommodate the crowds. Police direct the foot traffic, waving hands and blowing whistles. I'd wager there are a hundred thousand spectators coming out in honor of the fallen hero.

Vendors circle through the crowd, peddling their Lieutenant Mercury merchandise. T-shirts, hats, cookies, water bottles, and cupcakes are just some of the goods for sale. Most of the T-shirts have an image of Lieutenant Mercury with *Rest in Peace* stenciled underneath it.

Finding a lamppost, I scurry up it. The enormity of the crowd is breathtaking. There are so many people that I can't even see the street below—they completely blanket it.

In the distance is a stage, where Mystic holds a microphone. The four other remaining members of the Core sit behind her. Streak, wearing his red, skintight costume, taps his foot as if bored, but his super-accelerated ability to move makes his foot a blur. Rocket and Sling sit next to each other. I think about the night at the parking garage, and it angers me that these two phonies can sit on this stage and play the part of heroes. Rocket adjusts his mask, which causes him to accidentally nudge Roisin in the shoulder. She shoots him a look, but he's oblivious. I can see Mystic's lips move, but the words I hear through the sound system don't match up with them. I realize I'm so far away that there's a delay, so what she says doesn't sync with what I hear.

"Lieutenant Mercury was the best among us," Mystic is saying. "He had a dream years ago to assemble the best of the best to protect this great city. The remaining members of the Core will honor his deepest desire and continue to serve the citizens of Loganstin. His untimely death weighs heavily on my soul, as it does for my friends and teammates. I want to reassure each and every one of you in attendance here today that we—"

Without warning, she stops in mid-sentence. She looks into the crowd, scanning faces like a speed reader skimming the words in a novel. Her eyes stop, and while I can't be one hundred percent certain, it appears that she's staring at me.

Not diverting her eyes from my direction, Mystic lifts the microphone to her lips and says, "Please remain calm, but Lieutenant Mercury's killer is in this crowd, right now."

If Mystic wanted to incite the crowd, this achieves her goal. A murmur ripples through the spectators. The four seated members of the Core jump to their feet and move to Mystic's side, ready to launch into action at her command. If it weren't for the situation, they would look rather comical, striking the pose that's become a cliché for costumed crime fighters—fists held up, legs spread wide, searching dramatically for evil forces only they are capable of fighting.

"Apparently he wasn't aware I could read his mind," Mystic says. "I can't think of a better tribute than to apprehend the killer in front of all of you." She drops the microphone, but I don't wait around long enough to hear the noise this makes through the speaker system. I slide down the lamppost and hurry off into the wall of people.

The crowd grows more agitated. People are trampled, and I hear sirens in the distance. Riot police, wearing helmets and clutching shields, storm into the thick of things. As I shove my way through the throng, a couple of police officers raise their batons and savagely smack unruly agitators. The whole scene turns to chaos.

No matter which way I move, I'm traveling against the motion of the crowd. "Out of my way," I yell, but my voice is drowned out by the rising mayhem.

A path clears in the crowd, allowing the members of the Core to storm through. Mystic points her manicured finger at me. The other teammates look in my direction. Jumping into a procession of people moving away from the Core, I flow along with the crowd, struggling to remain on my feet. A shadow passes overhead. I can feel it following me as I zigzag along with the mob. I glance up and see him—Rocket. The eyes behind his mask are locked on me, like an eagle tracking its prey as he flies through the air above me. He points a finger at me, looks back over his shoulder, and yells, "The cretin is right here!"

Up ahead, I spot a subway entrance. I race toward it. I don't have to look up to know Rocket is still tracking me from above. Reaching the stairs, I take the steps three at a time. I feel a rush of air on my neck, and, out of the corner of my eye, see the soles of Rocket's boots shoot overhead.

"The elusive lad is going subterranean!" Rocket yells.

I jump over the gate and run past the people waiting in line. A couple of them yell at me to wait my turn, but I race ahead as fast as my legs will carry me. I'm out of breath and tired. I feel a hand clamp down on my shoulder and spin around, coming face-to-face with Eliza.

She grabs my hand and puts four syringes of Dr. Klaus's concoction into my palm. As she closes my fingers over them, she says, "Leave town and never come back." She disappears down the platform. She's left me to the wolves.

I'll need all the power I can get. I remove the cap from one needle and jam it through my shirt, into my stomach. Squeezing it tightly, I empty the blue concoction into myself and then toss the spent syringe. Finding someone with fear on the subway platform is as easy as eenie, meenie, miney, moe, and I power up.

I feel a whoosh of air move past us, kicking up discarded pieces of paper. All I see is a blur, and I know it's Streak. He stops right in front of me. Recognition bubbles to the surface and comes to a boil. "You!"

Launching myself into the air, I land in the middle of the subway tracks, hitting the ground running. Exploding like a bullet out of the barrel of a gun, I run into the subway tunnel. Streak zips after me, closing the gap rather quickly. Digging deep, I crank up the juice, speeding away as fast as I can. The subway tunnel winds beneath the city like an underground river that cuts its way through the earth.

I'm not certain, but I'm pretty sure I hear Streak cursing. There are plenty of fliers who can travel faster than him, but that's in the air. He's been the undisputed champ on the ground for years. I'm sure he doesn't like me challenging his superiority. But I wonder how long I'll be able to keep this up. If it weren't for Dr. Klaus's concoction, I'd be spent.

A bright light shines up ahead, signaling an approaching train. Streak is behind me. I can feel him barreling down. I slow down, allowing him to get closer. The fingertips of his outstretched hand brush my shoulder. All his focus is on catching me. But all my focus is on the approaching train, its lights blinding as the distance closes rapidly.

Streak's hand lands on my shoulder, tightens. "Gotcha!"

Timing it perfectly, I jump just as the train threatens to mow me down. I arc high into the air and land on the top of the train. Streak yells, followed by the sound of crushing metal. He bounces off the front of the train and slams into the platform. The impact causes the concrete to crack, fracturing like a web. Chunks of concrete break away and fall on him.

Running along the train's roof, I pace it so I remain stationary in the tunnel. The train rushes under my feet until I leap into the air as the train ends. My feet land between the tracks. The train continues down the tunnel.

The sound of whimpering draws my attention to Streak, who lies in a fetal position off to the side of the tracks. He moans as he rocks back and forth, clutching his leg. "You broke my leg!" he snaps. He shoots me a nasty look and tries to get to his feet. He can push himself up, but he grimaces as he attempts to put weight on the injured leg. Hopping toward me, he says, "I'm gonna kill you!"

"There's been a misunderstanding," I say.

Favoring his hurt leg, he jumps at me. "I'm gonna enjoy hearin' you scream!" Giving up on explaining myself, I turn and zip away, leaving him hobbling in the middle of the subway tunnel.

The tracks eventually move aboveground to the depot, where the trains get refueled, repaired, and stored for the night. My heart drops when I see the other members of the Core—Mystic, Rocket, and Sling—standing shoulder-to-shoulder in the middle of the tracks. My feet dig into the gravel and I come to a grinding stop. My shirt and jeans are shredded and in tatters, and my shoes are melting on my feet.

"Marvin, you've gone far enough," Mystic says. She presses her palm against the side of her head and grimaces, like she's suffering from a migraine. But then her facial features soften and her eyes focus clearly on me. I can tell by her face that she's in my brain, piecing my memories together like a jigsaw puzzle.

"You sonavabitch!" Sling yells, lunging toward me, his weightlifter's costume tightly hugging his enormous thighs.

"Sling, no!" Mystic yells.

But Sling is charging me, lowering his head to ram me. Veins in his neck bulge like large worms, and his fists are clenched so tightly his knuckles are white. I speed past him in a blur. Rocket launches into the air, but I easily zoom past him, moving so quickly it causes him to wobble in flight like a kite without a tail. He smacks into the side of a train.

Running as fast as I can, I follow the subway tracks back into a tunnel. As I disappear into the darkness, I hear someone calling my name, and it lingers like an echo.

TWENTY-FIVE

There are highway workers in vests and hardhats working on the freeway, near the entrance to the concrete cave. I can see them under the glow of artificial lights. Concealing myself, I watch from a distance. My power has faded, or I'd just zip past them and enter my old home without them even seeing me. After the events of the night, I'm seriously paranoid. I jump at every noise, afraid a member of the Core has found me. I just want to get indoors and seal myself away until I can figure out what to do.

I approach a tree that's nestled by the on-ramp. Safely out of sight of the road workers, I get down on my hands and knees to brush aside dead leaves and dirt. When I find the manhole cover, I dislodge the heavy lid, push it aside, and climb inside the hole.

It's dark inside the manhole, and the air is stagnant like a sealed tomb. I descend a ladder covered in rust and grime. Reaching the bottom, I make my way through the utility corridor, following the bundles of electric lines and fiber-optic cables that lead me to a metal grille. Getting down on my knees, I dig my fingertips into the grille and try to pull it loose, but I can't get it. It's rusted shut. I pull on the grille until my fingers bleed, finally ripping it off.

On my elbows and knees, I shimmy into the passage. My skin rubs raw as I creep onward like a caterpillar. I stop a couple of times to rest, but force myself to keep moving. The sooner I'm out of this tunnel, the better.

Up ahead, light shines through a grille in the floor. A wave of relief washes over me as I approach it. Rolling onto my back, I look up through the floor of our kitchen. I push up on the grille and hear it clank onto the floor. I pull myself up.

The soft flickering of light from the television reflects on the outside wall. I wipe my sweaty palms on the front of my jeans. My mouth is dry, and I try to swallow, but it gets stuck in the back of my throat. The back of Kent's mushy head pokes over the sofa's headrest. *It's not too late*, I think. He hasn't seen me yet. I could disappear without him knowing I was here. But I don't have anyone else I can turn to for help.

"Hey," I mumble.

Kent jumps to his feet and swivels around to face me. "Dude, you scared the hell outta me!" he says. He ambles around the sofa and gives me a big hug. "Man, Marvin, it's good to see you."

I hug him back and say, "Same here."

"Crazy about Mercury, huh?" he says. "So, how's it going?"

"Um ... not good," I mumble, not knowing where to start.

Yvonne steps into the room, ignoring me as she plops

down in front of the television. I wait for her to say something, or at the very least acknowledge me, but she doesn't.

Kent gives me a halfhearted smile and says, "Don't mind her. She's still coming around."

"I didn't know where else to go," I say. "I'm in big trouble."

"What're you talking about?" Kent asks. "What kind of trouble?"

"I killed Lieutenant Mercury."

Kent laughs as Yvonne finally looks at me, studying my face. I wilt under the scrutiny. Kent stops laughing and says, "Oh, wait, this isn't a joke?"

"Eliza and I were attacked by this guy," I say. "I didn't know who he was, but I found out later it was Darren Campbell."

"He was the most powerful clean ever," Kent says.

"Eliza shot me up with a couple of vials of this stuff," I say, shrugging. I pat my pocket and feel the three remaining syringes inside. "It happened so quickly. I didn't know what was going on."

Kent appears to lose his balance and plops down in the chair. My confession is too heavy a weight to carry.

"All I ever wanted out of life was to help people," I say. "I failed to help my mother. I thought I could make up for that if I could join the Core. So when Eliza said I could try out for the team, it finally felt like I had a shot at redemption."

Nobody says anything for what seems like forever. Yvonne's fierce eyes pierce me. Before I can say anything, she storms off.

Kent wants to say something, and he starts a couple of times but changes his mind, finally giving up.

"Do me a favor," I say, staring at where Yvonne stormed

off. "Watch after her and keep a low profile." I head toward the exit.

I halfway expect Kent to stop me and say that everything will be okay. We'll figure it out. We'll get through this together.

But he doesn't. He probably respects me too much to lie.

TWENTY-SIX

The sky is clear and the sun is warm. It's a nice day, but it might as well be pouring rain, the way I feel. I haven't slept a wink. I don't know where I'm going and I don't know what will happen to me. I can't be angry with my friends. I abandoned them for a tryout. Not a spot on the team, but just a tryout with the hope of making the cut.

I walk aimlessly, all the way into Little Saigon, wallowing the whole way in my misery. Street peddlers hawk their goods in the middle of the road, making it impossible for automobiles to navigate the streets. More business is conducted on the bustling asphalt roadways than in the brick-and-mortar stores. I pass a man pushing a wooden cart with dead chickens hung upside down by their feet. A woman sells pirated DVDs on a blanket spread out in the middle of an intersection.

Weaving in and out of the noisy vendors, I head over to an electronics store with a window display of small televisions stacked on top of each other. All of the televisions are tuned to a basketball game. I used to watch this basketball team with my father. It seems like a lifetime ago. Our small-market team has never won a championship. Ever. I once asked my father why he always rooted for a team that never won. He'd smiled and replied, "It's easy to root for a winner, but it takes integrity to root for someone who's outgunned yet stays in the game to the bitter end."

This is the only thing of value my father ever gave me.

Without warning, the basketball game is replaced by a news report. A police sketch, which is unmistakably me, fills the screen. I feel like an 18-wheeler just hit me as I stare at my face. A crawl line proclaiming *Channel Two News, Breaking Report* runs along the top of the screen, just above the illustration of me. Wanting to hear what's said, I race into the electronics store.

"This is a police sketch of one of the suspects wanted in the murder of Lieutenant Mercury," the anchorman says.

One of the suspects?

"Authorities say this boy should be considered powerful and very dangerous. Do not attempt to apprehend him. If any of our viewers has any information regarding his whereabouts, please call the police immediately," the anchorman says.

The newscast then cuts to an interview with Sling and Rocket. They stand outside the Core Mansion. "The Core has been collaborating with local law enforcement agencies to help solve this heinous crime as quickly as possible," Rocket says.

A reporter off-camera asks, "Do you have any idea how many people are involved?"

"We have reason to believe there are three individuals involved," Sling says. "Maybe more."

The two costumed heroes end the interview and walk

into the mansion, leaving behind a barrage of questions from the media.

A woman holding a microphone steps in front of the camera. "That was members of the Core taking questions regarding leads in the murder of Lieutenant Mercury. The Core and the police are asking for the public's help in bringing the people responsible to justice."

As if my image wasn't enough, up comes a mug shot of Yvonne. I feel again like I've been hit in the stomach. An illustration, which I can only assume is supposed to be Kent, flashes onscreen too. If I wasn't so freaked out, I'd laugh. His face looks like a plastic doll left too close to a heater. While it might not look like him, it certainly captures his essence.

"These three dirties are wanted for questioning," the newscaster says. "Again, they should be considered powerful and dangerous."

The crowd gathers around me. All eyes are on the televisions, transfixed. I cut through the people toward the store exit, careful to avoid eye contact with anyone. I'm almost to the door when I bump into someone. "Watch where you're going," the man says.

Not glancing up, I say, "Sorry." I keep on moving.

"Hey, it's him!" I hear the man yell, pointing a finger at me. "It's that kid on the TV!"

As if on cue, the crowd of thirty people or so turn from the televisions and stare at me. "It is him!" someone else yells. The group moves toward me. A chorus of voices rings out: "Don't let him get away!" and "Let's get 'im!"

I run out the door and try to put distance between the angry mob and myself.

"Stop him!" a woman screams. "Someone stop that boy!"

"He's the one who killed Lieutenant Mercury!"

I run through the streets dodging pedestrians and vehicles, their horns blaring. Sprinting through an alley, I come out the other side and barely avoid slamming into a police squad car, which brakes and comes to a jolting stop. My hands rest on the hood of the car as I stare at the two startled officers inside. Making eye contact with the man behind the wheel, I read his lips as he swears at me. For a split second I think maybe they don't know who I am, but then I read recognition on both faces. "It's him," the driver tells his partner.

I back away from the police car and sprint off. Behind me, I hear tires squeal as the patrol car closes in. I run up the stoop leading into an apartment building right as a little girl carrying a jump rope steps outside. Catching the door before it closes, I dash inside. "You're supposed to enter a code to come in!" the little girl yells.

Ignoring her, I slam the door shut as the police cruiser jumps up on the curb, screeching to a stop. I run up the flight of stairs. When I turn the corner onto the second floor, I see two elderly men wearing shorts, socks, and flip-flops. They sit at a folding table in the hall, playing cards and watching a small portable television. The breaking news is still on the screen. One of the men points a bony finger at me as I run up the stairs again. "It's that kid!"

Reaching the fifth floor, I stop long enough to look up the middle of the staircase. I figure there are at least six more floors to go until I reach the roof. The two police officers are a few flights below.

On the top floor, I find the door locked. Backing up, I

get a running start and ram my shoulder into it, breaking it off its hinges and dumping myself unceremoniously on top of it. I scramble to my feet and run to the edge of the roof. The street is eleven stories below, and more squad cars are pulling up to the building. Officers unholster their sidearms as they get into position.

"Freeze! Put your hands up!" I turn around and find the two police officers pointing their guns at me. Their faces are red and sweaty. "Don't take another step!"

Reaching into my pocket, I remove a syringe of the blue go-go juice and slam the needle into my thigh. Squeezing it to release the concoction into my bloodstream, I probe for fear. It's a regular smorgasbord of the stuff up here. Both cops are practically mass-producing it.

Absorbing it, I feel power course through my body. Time seems to slow down, and everything becomes clear, like a veil has been lifted. One of the cops pulls back the hammer on his gun with his thumb. The click rings in my ears, muffling all other noise. I jump up on the roof's ledge.

"Step away from the ledge!" the other cop yells.

I launch myself into the air with all my might. I fly into the sky, hurtling toward the adjacent rooftop. For a brief moment, it almost feels like I'm a flier, streaking across the skyline, the wind biting at my face, causing my eyes to tear.

I didn't plan my jump well. I'd hoped to leapfrog to safety, but I'm dangerously close to overshooting my landing. As I reach the crest of ascent, I'm already more than halfway over the adjacent rooftop and it looks like I'm certain to overshoot it entirely. Losing balance in midair, I wave my arms in a feeble attempt to steady myself.

As I begin what will not be a pleasant descent, I hear a high-pitched sound that resembles air escaping from a tire. I don't know where the noise is coming from, but it's getting louder. Something approaches me in a blur. When it's nearly on top of me, I see the unmistakable mask of Rocket. Unable to redirect myself, I'm powerless to move out of his way. He speeds past me, smacking the side of my body and sending me sprawling. White-hot pain shoots through me as I plummet out of control to the rooftop, like a bird picked off by a hunter's gun.

"It would have behooved you to remain on the ground," Rocket yells, circling around.

I crash onto the roof, landing hard on my back. The impact forces all the air in my lungs out in a rush. Rocket streaks across the sky above me and then makes another large turn.

Everything is upside down and the world is spinning. Out of the corner of my eye, I spot Rocket flying a few feet above the rooftop, speeding toward me with his fist cocked. I jump toward him, sidestepping at the last minute and hooking his arm with my own. I use his momentum to whip him around and sling him high into the air. He nearly crashes into the adjacent building. He slows to a stop, steadies himself, and shoots back toward me, arms stretched forward like twin battering rams.

I brace for impact. He strikes with full force into my body. It feels like his fists go right through me. My insides feel like they're puréed. The impact sends the two of us flying in separate directions. He crashes against a wall, sending bricks tumbling to the ground. I'm nearly blasted off the rooftop but I manage to grab a ledge with one hand, which keeps me from tumbling to the street below.

Even with the vial of Dr. Klaus's concoction, I can feel my power draining. I'm losing strength. Maybe my body is building up a tolerance to the stuff.

Hanging on for dear life, I dangle. I try to pull myself up on the ledge but don't have the strength. Things go from bad to worse when Rocket peers over the ledge, smiles at me, and says, "You're like Icarus, who flew too close to the sun."

He extends a hand, and for a moment I think he's offering me his help. But he grabs my wrist and takes off flying again. The ground disappears far below us as we speed past the arriving television helicopters.

"Where are you taking me?" I yell.

He doesn't offer an explanation. With a firm grip on my wrist, he flies over the city. As he follows the Loganstin River, I realize he's taking me to the Core Mansion.

This is confirmed when he comes to a stop in midair, directly over the mansion. "Buddha said: Even death is not to be feared by one who has lived wisely."

"I don't understand a word you're saying," I snap.

Rocket pulls me up so we're face-to-face. "Lad, you have not acted wisely," he says with a sneer. Then he lets go.

TWENTY-SEVEN

Everything is black, and I can't even tell if my eyes are open. I try to raise a hand to my face, but I can't. *Where am I?*

A woman's voice answers from the darkness. "In our mansion," she says, as smooth as silk. "The Core Mansion."

Mystic's face emerges over me. So, she's reading my mind.

"Yes, I'm reading your mind," she says. "I've been probing around in your head while you slept for the last thirty hours. And let me just say, you're one interesting young man."

Lifting my head as much as I can, I find myself bound to a gurney with thick leather straps that securely fasten my ankles, wrists, and torso to the hard surface.

"I extracted the location of your home in the overpass," Mystic continues. "But once we got there, your friends were nowhere to be found."

I smile, happy that Yvonne and Kent bolted. Good for them.

"I know now that your friends weren't involved," she says, "but my colleagues have painted themselves into a corner on that one, so we're going to have to bring them in."

Even though they're innocent?

"It's more complicated than being innocent or not."

"Please stop reading my mind," I say. "It's freaking me out."

"You should be grateful I've been probing your head," Mystic says, "because I've discovered the truth about Eliza's involvement with this whole debacle." She slips away and I hear her flip a switch. We're bathed in a flood of bright light. Mystic wears a lot of makeup, but it can't cover up the wrinkles around her piercing blue eyes or the tiny scars on her cheeks. This just reinforces the idea that has become more and more clear to me recently—up close, nobody is perfect.

She pulls a chair over and takes a seat, crossing her legs and studying me for a moment before saying, "You were not trying out for the Core. I'm sorry. I know how much that meant to you."

It feels like I've just had a winning lotto ticket snatched out from under my nose, or discovered that a wonderful dream is just a dream and didn't really happen.

"Eliza didn't have the authority to extend that offer," Mystic adds.

It's like all my hopes and dreams have come crashing down around me. I gave up everything I hold dear for a lie. I quit my job, quit my friends, and played fast and loose with my sense of right and wrong—for absolutely nothing.

"Marvin, I think you're being a little hard on yourself," Mystic says. "You had no way of knowing."

"I should've known," I say. "It was too good to be true. Something like that doesn't happen to a nobody like me."

"Marvin, I think Eliza underestimated you, which is something I'll never do."

"Where is she?"

"No clue. She upped and vanished," Mystic says. "None of this would've happened if I could read her mind. I have difficulty piecing together the thoughts of people with mental health disorders. She's been diagnosed with Schizotypal personality disorder."

"What's that?"

"She experiences psychotic episodes. She's a troubled girl."

"Tell me something I don't know," I mumble.

Mystic glances back at the closed door. She leans in close and whispers, "So, about the Core—"

"You all belong in prison," I say.

She puts a finger to her lips. "Shush. Keep it down. Someone might be listening."

"I was so wrong about you guys. I thought you were heroes."

Mystic appears to consider this. "I haven't been a hero since the summer of 2008. That was when I went to the other side, crossed the line. I've been trying to get back ever since."

"But why?"

She motions around the room and says, "Who do you think paid for this place, this mansion? Or pays for the fuel for the Flame of Truth? Or all those ridiculous vehicles in the garage?"

"I don't know."

"We do," she says. "We pay. The Core. And crime fighting is pro bono work. It's done without pay."

"Then how do you make money?" I ask.

"That's the billion-dollar question," she says. "When I joined the Core, we got a stipend from the federal government.

It wasn't much, but between that and getting Loganstin to pony up for the construction of the Core Mansion, we did all right. Then the economy took a nosedive. There were budget cuts across the board. Our funds actually dried up altogether. It didn't make sense for the federal government to fund a group that pretty much only operated in one city, but Loganstin wasn't going to offer up any more money after coughing up the funds to build our mansion. The Core was broke."

She explained that the only money to be made in this line of work was being made by the criminals. Crime fighting doesn't pay the bills.

"What Darren suggested we do to support ourselves made a lot of sense at the time," she says. "We'd fund ourselves by confiscating the criminals' money."

"You robbed them."

"We considered it a tax for services rendered. We ate what we killed, so to speak. If we apprehended a drug dealer, why should the police department get to confiscate the money? The Core did the work, so shouldn't we get the financial rewards?"

I don't know if Mystic is waiting for me to reply, but I don't say anything. I don't know what to say.

"I know it's hard for you to hear this. It's hard for me to admit it." Mystic looks down at the floor. "A few years back, we got word of a large drug deal happening in the harbor. All of us were there for that one. The whole team. After everything was said and done that day, fifteen people were dead. And there was an entire shipping container filled with black tar heroin. But no cash." She shrugs, as if giving a response to a question only she can hear. "Merc wasn't going to leave empty-handed."

"You took the drugs."

She looks up at me, as if surprised to find me bound to the gurney and listening to her. She nods her head. "The whole container. Merc hoisted it into the air and flew it here to the island. It took us nearly a month to sell it all. Pocketed nearly a hundred million. That was the summer of 2008. That's when the dream died. Everything was different after that."

Everything's been building to this moment for the last few weeks. The clues and red flags were there. Some I saw, but others I ignored. I'd hoped it was all wrong. I tried to convince myself I was just being paranoid. I wanted more than anything to discover that it was just a big misunderstanding—or, at the very least, that it was only Eliza who was responsible. But the criminal activity went all the way to the top. All the way up to Lieutenant Mercury.

Police Chief Earl Wooden was wrong about the Core. They're not ceremonial crime fighters—they're nothing more than a cartel in tights.

"It wasn't always like this," Mystic repeats. "In the beginning, we did right by the citizens of Loganstin. We were heroes," she says.

"But that hardly matters now," I say.

"Yeah," she mumbles.

"What do you know about Mercury falling out of the sky into a house, killing a husband and wife? This was about seven years ago. Their young daughter survived."

She looks at me. I don't have to be told that she's foraging around in my head like a raccoon in a garbage can. "Her name is Yvonne," she says. "She's the one who drugged Streak."

I curse myself for allowing her to pickpocket my mind.

"Don't worry. It's our little secret. Streak's an asshole. God knows I'd drug him if I could get away with it. But to answer your question, yes, that's how Yvonne's parents died. The Mercury-industrial complex went into overdrive to contain that story." Mystic spots a smudge on her costume and tries to scratch it away with her fingernail. "There's a whole industry out there that benefits, both monetarily and politically, with the Core operating. There's too much on the line to allow something like killing Yvonne's parents to ruin a good thing."

"Where does Eliza fit into this whole scenario?" I ask.

"She tried to circumvent the system, leapfrogging to the head of the class. But that's what we get for allowing a sociopath to join the team. She'll be dealt with."

"What's going to happen now?" I ask.

"Oh, haven't I been clear? You're going to join the Core," Mystic says.

"What?"

"Eliza's spot on the team has just opened up. Think of all the adventures you're going to have! Your dream has come true."

"After everything you've just told me, why on earth would you think I'd want to join?" I say. "You're all corrupt. You're worse than the criminals you put away."

"But you and I are going to change the Core from the inside," Mystic says. "We can make it better. We can actually be the team people think we are." She stands up. "I'll give you some time to mull it over." She walks to the door, her high heels clicking on the floor.

"What if I say no?"

"Right now, you're wanted for the murder of the most beloved man to ever wear a cape."

"You're threatening me?"

"Just think about it." She flips off the lights as she steps into the hall, shutting the door with a clang. The sound of the lock sliding into place echoes throughout the room.

In the darkness, I struggle against my restraints, which hold me firmly in place. Letting my mind probe for fear, I find nothing. If there's anybody close by, they're not scared. Without my power, I'm helpless to free myself. I'm stuck like a rat in a trap. Wherever Yvonne and Kent are, I hope they don't surface. The best thing for them is to get out of the city and never look back.

"Pssd. Maavin."

I swivel my head to look toward the barred window. "Who's there?"

"Id's mae ... Keed."

"Where?"

"Bay dea windoo," he whispers. A stream of goo drips onto the floor. It kind of looks like spoiled milk, clumpy and uneven, as it flows over the windowsill. The sound of the dripping stops, and no sooner than it does, Kent forms out of the puddle of goo on the floor. He emerges by the side of the gurney, smiling through his limp flesh. "I've come to the rescue."

"How'd you know I was here?" I ask.

"We watched Rocket fly you away from the rooftop, on television," he says.

"Um ... Kent," I mumble, "are you naked?"

He glances down the front of his body and smiles. "Yeah."

"Why?"

"I just dripped my way in here. How am I going to do that with clothes?"

The lock on the door slides open.

"You've got to get out of here. Right now," I whisper.

"Not without you," Kent says, looking for a place to hide. But there isn't any. The room is empty except for the gurney and chair. He crosses the room and stands in front of the wall, running his hand over it. As he leans flat against it, arms and legs outstretched, his flesh spreads across the surface as if a rolling pin is flattening him. He melts into the cracks and pores of the wall, like water being absorbed by a sponge.

Just as he vanishes from sight, a flood of light enters from outside, but is quickly gone as the door shuts again.

Streak limps toward me. He's wearing a leg brace. "Well, well, well," he says, smirking. "What do we have here?" He removes a tiny silver flask, unscrews the cap, and takes a plug. "So, your name's Marvin, huh? Marvin. Maaaarvin. Maaarrr-viiiinn," he says, as if taking my name out on a test drive. He takes another drink and screws the cap back on, replacing the flask inside a pocket in his red suit.

"What do you want?" I say.

"An apology, to start with."

"For what?"

He starts to laugh, a little too loudly. "For what? *For what?* You killed Mercury!"

"There's been a big misunderstanding."

"Liar!" he screams.

"I...okay...I'm sorry, then," I say. "Sorry. I'm really super sorry."

He's close enough that I can smell the booze on his breath. "Oh, it doesn't work like that. An eye for an eye." He removes a box cutter from his pocket. With his thumb, he extends the blade. He slides the dull side of the blade across my cheek. "This is gonna hurt."

Kent emerges out of the wall, peeling off like wallpaper. His body inflates and takes shape as he tiptoes toward Streak, who's pulling back his arm, poised to jab the blade into me. "This is for Mercury!"

Before Streak can slice me, Kent jumps into the air, spreading out like a blanket and wrapping Streak up. The Core member struggles to get out, but he's like a fish caught in a net. The more he struggles, the more Kent appears to ensnare him, until Streak goes limp.

When Kent removes himself, Streak collapses to the floor, the blade clanking out of his hand. Kent's form reshapes back to normal. He bends down and retrieves the box cutter, using the sharp blade to cut the straps that hold me.

"Thanks, Kent," I say.

The light from the hall outside floods into the cell as the door swings open. Mystic scurries back into the room. "We don't have much time," she whispers, glancing at my friend. "Hi, Kent."

"Um ... hi," he says.

Mystic does a double take at Streak lying in a heap on the cold floor.

"He's just taking a little snooze," Kent says.

"The rest of the Core will be here in a minute," she says. "I'm afraid of what they'll do to you if they find you here."

"I'm getting Marvin out of here, one way or the other," Kent says.

"Trust me, if I'd wanted to stop you, I would've tipped off my teammates when you set foot on the island," she says.

"You knew I was here?"

"Of course I did. I was probing your mind even before you floated to shore."

Kent stands up straight, puffs his chest out, and swaggers toward her. "Probed my mind, huh? Did you find anything you liked?"

If Mystic notices that Kent is naked, she doesn't show it. "Your thoughts belong in the gutter."

"I bet you'd like that," he says, giving her a wink.

"You need to find some proof of your innocence or you're all sunk," she says, motioning us to follow her as she heads toward the door. She points down the darkened corridor. "Go that way. It leads outside."

"Why are you helping us?" I ask.

She stares at me for moment before saying, "Think about my offer, Marvin." And with that, she disappears down the dark hall.

We find the door, but it's locked and won't budge when I yank on it. There are bars on it. Standing on my tiptoes, I see the gentle slope that leads to the Loganstin River, just out of reach outside.

Pushing me aside, Kent says, "I'll handle this." He presses his hand against the doorknob. His hand liquefies and flows into the lock. He makes a face as he concentrates. "Almost … almost … almost there." Something clicks, and he rotates his wrist counterclockwise. The ooze retreats out of the lock, forming back into his hand. "Ta-da!" he says, opening the door.

I get a whiff of the putrid body of water below as we approach the river's edge. "I don't know if I can swim across. It's far," I say.

"Swim? You don't have to swim," Kent says, his body melting into a pile and then reforming into a bowl—a lopsided, uneven, and wobbly bowl, but a bowl nonetheless. His face, stretched out like taffy, is on the outside to better see where he's going. I can't help but laugh.

"Wha ou laafin ad?"

"You made yourself into a boat," I say.

"Stoop laafin, ou jerd," he says. "Ush mae endu waadur."

I shove off the shore and jump in, landing harder than I intended and causing Kent to grunt. "Sorry," I say.

"Bea caaful," he grumbles. "Sdurd paadlen."

I lean over the side and use both hands, awkwardly paddling like a dog.

TWENTY-EIGHT

Finally managing to get around the island and to the other side of the river, we reach shore. As I jump out of the bowl-shaped Kent, Yvonne runs toward us. "What took you guys so long?"

"Yvonne, you came too?" I say.

"Yeah."

I pull Kent onto shore. His body melts into a shapeless blob before retaking human form. Yvonne tosses his clothes at him, which he hurries to put on. "That water is freaking cold," he grumbles.

"Thanks for coming, Yvonne. I'm so sorry. For everything."

She looks at me for a long time before saying, "You bring out the best in Kent and me. You make us want to be better people."

It takes me a moment to realize my mouth is hanging open. Kent finishes getting dressed, but he's too embarrassed to look me in the eyes. Yvonne shuffles her weight from foot to foot and rubs the back of her neck.

"You were our conscience," she says. "The two of us didn't

always do the right thing, but we always felt bad because we knew that you wouldn't approve."

"Really?" I say.

"Yeah," Kent says.

"Why do you think I finally gave up getting junkies high?"

"I thought it was because of the little girl. Harry."

Yvonne nods her head. "She certainly helped my decision, but it was mostly because of you."

I'm overcome. I clear my throat and say, "I had no—"

She punches me hard on the shoulder. "So don't ever bail on us again!"

I rub my shoulder. "Ouch!"

Yvonne hugs me, and the embrace lingers. As she pulls away, she asks, "What happened out there?"

"Eliza's vanished," I say. "And Mystic offered me a spot on the Core—Eliza's spot."

"Really?" Kent says.

"I told her thanks but no thanks," I say. A smile replaces the scowl Yvonne's been wearing the past week. "I'm sorry I doubted your story about your parents. Mystic told me it was all true."

Tears well up in Yvonne's eyes.

"I know what it's like to have a parent ripped from you," I say. "But unlike you, I could've done something to stop it."

My friends stare at me but don't say a word.

"My father killed my mother. The argument sounded just like all the hundreds of others they'd had. But this time my father was drunker than normal, and they fought about me going to the Power Aversion Program. My mom didn't want me to go. This time, when he struck my mom, he didn't stop.

And I did nothing to stop him. I hid in my room and tried to block out the noise."

"Marvin, it's not your fault," Yvonne says. "You were just a kid."

"No," I say, "I could've stopped him. My powers had just developed. But I didn't know why or how it was happening. I didn't know that it was fed by fear. It scared me. I thought I was a freak. But I could've stopped my father. I should've stopped him. Not a day goes by that I don't wish I could go back and find the courage to act. I swore I'd never make that mistake again. I will never, ever again live with the regret of not acting. It's the least I can do to honor my mother."

Yvonne takes my hand and squeezes it, then wipes her moist eyes with her other hand.

"We should probably get out of here," I say, heading away from the shoreline.

"Where're we going?" Kent asks, following me.

"We're going to Eliza's safe house."

"Why are we going to that skank's place?" Yvonne asks.

"To check her videos," I say. "I should've thought of it sooner."

"Videos?" Kent says.

Heading away from the river, we make our way through the shrubs and underbrush and step out onto the road. "She films everything," I say.

We run across the busy street, to a gas station with a pay phone. I open the phone book to get a number for a cab company. Dropping two quarters into the slot, I dial the number and order a taxi.

"Maybe we should just run," Yvonne says. "Leave this mess behind us. Go far away."

"I'm not running," I say. "They'll never leave us alone. This isn't a problem that'll just go away. I'm not about to let you two go down because of my stupid mistake."

The taxi pulls into the gas station parking lot and the three of us pile inside. Yvonne and I sit in the back, holding hands. It doesn't seem strange or awkward. It feels right.

Kent notices our intertwined hands and says, "Get a room."

The taxi driver glances back at us in the rearview mirror, his eyes widening as he gets an eyeful of Kent. Yvonne notices this and leans across me toward Kent. In a hushed voice, she says, "Cover your face."

Kent's limp fingers rise to his sagging face. "Oops." He pulls the hood of his jacket over his head. The taxi driver continues to stare at him in the rearview mirror. "Watch the road," Kent tells him.

The cabbie raises an eyebrow when I tell him to deposit us near the safe house. Yvonne pays the guy. I lead my friends into the building and up the staircase. "Our concrete cave is paradise next to this place," Yvonne says.

Reaching the top of the stairs, the first thing I notice is that the front door to Eliza's apartment is wide open. Putting my finger to my lips, I motion for my friends to be quiet. We silently make our way in. On first glance, the place appears to be untouched. I lead my friends down the hall into the Roisin shrine.

"Is this her stuff?" Kent asks.

"Yeah," I say, heading over to the closet.

"I was wrong," Yvonne says. "She's not a skank. She's an egomaniacal skank."

I punch in the code on the keypad, the light turns from red to green, and the lock slides open. I swing open the closet door. There's nothing inside but the computer and the data sticker device. The two hard drives are gone. No DVDs, no memory cards. Nothing. Zip. Nada.

"It's gone," I say. "It's all gone."

Pushing me aside, Yvonne sits down at the computer. "Don't get all whiny yet. Let's see if she forgot to clear out the cache." She types in a series of commands, opening folders and inspecting the contents of the hard drive.

"I didn't know you knew about computers," I say.

"There's a lot about me that you don't know," Yvonne says, opening a folder and inspecting the icons. "These look like video files." She clicks on one, opening the media player. Kent and Yvonne lean in and try to make out the blurry video.

My heart drops. It's the footage of Eliza and me at the dam.

Reaching over Yvonne, I take the mouse and click to stop the footage. "That's nothing," I say.

"What was that?" Kent asks. "I couldn't make it out."

"Nothing," I say, dragging the icon and depositing it into the recycle bin. "Try another one."

Yvonne gives me a strange look before clicking on another video file. The footage plays. It takes me a second, but I recognize the alley behind the Chinese restaurant. "This is it," I say.

The video shows Eliza and me hurrying into the alley. My backside fills the frame. Eliza looks around, and her eyes stare directly at the camera. She moves me out of the way and says, "Marvin, stand right here."

We see Darren Campbell walking toward us. It's hard to hear, but he says, "Roisin, what's going on?"

And then all hell breaks loose. The man charges me, sending me into a stack of wooden crates.

"Damn!" Kent says.

Eliza shoots Darren with a blast from her eyes, but he grabs her and hoists her into the air, slapping her across the face. We watch as I barrel into Darren, which launches him off his feet and straight into the air.

Eliza and I run down the alley, out of the frame of the camera, but the footage switches to a different camera and angle. "How many cameras were there?" Yvonne asks.

"I don't know," I say.

The footage shows Darren kicking me repeatedly. "Who are you?" he yells.

It's hard to watch, but I make myself.

From another angle, Darren flies inches over my head. I grab him and swing him into the ground. He smacks against it, headfirst.

Both my friends gasp, and I close my eyes.

None of us say anything as the footage shows Eliza and me running out of the alley. The camera stays on Darren, lying there motionless. As the footage continues to play, Darren stirs and groans. His eyes blink repeatedly.

"He's alive," I say.

Darren rolls over onto his stomach. He spits out a mouthful of blood. Eliza steps into frame, standing over him on the ground. He looks up at her. In a weakened voice, he says, "You're going to have to do better than that." He laughs as he pushes himself up, rising to his knees. "You'll be nothing but a stain when I'm done with you."

Eliza remains rooted in place, glaring down at him. "That's why I used Marvin, to wear you down so this would work," she says.

"So what would work?" he asks.

Eliza's eyes glow as her power charges up. He just stares at her defiantly, as if silently daring her to do it. A bolt of energy erupts out of her eyes and strikes him in the face. His head is violently tossed to the side, and the sound of something snapping, like a branch in a heavy wind, echoes through the computer's speakers. He drops to the ground.

"Oh my god," Yvonne mutters.

Eliza pokes her foot against Darren's body. He doesn't stir. She turns and walks toward the camera. We see her hands come into the frame and pick it up. The footage shows her face for just a second before it goes black.

"She killed him," Kent says.

Yvonne looks around the desk, under it, and at the back of the computer. "Ta-da," she says, reaching behind the computer and fiddling with something. She holds up something between her thumb and finger.

"What's that?" Kent asks.

"It's a data sticker," I say. It's not the one retrieved from the blackmailers. It looks older and well used, judging by the scuffs.

"Correctamundo," Yvonne says, sticking it on the scanner. She drags and drops the video file we just watched, copying it onto the data sticker. The device spins and chirps. She removes the sticker and hands it to me. "I'm sure there are countless people who would know what to do with this footage."

"But which one will help clear our name?" Kent asks.

That's the million-dollar question, I think. At this point, I don't know who we can trust.

"First things first," I say, heading into the hall. My friends follow behind me. "We've got to—"

The windowpane shatters into a thousand pieces. Glass rains down. The three of us drop to the floor. A bullet whizzes overhead, striking the nearby wall.

Crawling on my belly, I say, "This way." We race down the hallway and into the bedroom. Pulling the curtains aside, I peek out. "Oh, man."

Outside, three large SWAT team vans are parked in front of the building. Two dozen men decked out in Kevlar vests and toting some heavy firepower have set up a perimeter. Chief of Police Earl Wooden storms around barking orders. He points to a location on the rooftop of the adjacent building. I spot three men with sniper rifles looking through the scopes at our apartment.

One of Wooden's lackeys scurries out and puts a bullhorn into his boss's outstretched hand. The device squawks as the chief puts it to his lips, which elicits a grimace. Trying again, Wooden speaks into the mouthpiece. "This is Chief of Police Earl Wooden of the Loganstin Police Department. The building is surrounded. Come out with your hands locked behind your heads."

"What are we going to do?" Kent mumbles.

I flip on the television and a crystal-clear image appears, showing a breaking news story. SWAT team members are in position, pointing their high-powered rifles at our building. They all look pretty serious and kind of pissed.

"This is bad," Yvonne says.

The sound of feedback from a megaphone screeches from outside. It goes silent, and then a voice bellows, "I repeat: You are surrounded! Come out with your hands locked behind your heads!"

On the television, we can see Wooden, bullhorn to his lips, now standing safely behind a squad car. "You have one minute to give up peacefully," he says, his voice booming, "or we're coming in."

"One minute," Yvonne mumbles. "Not a lot of time."

The heavily armed SWAT team prepares to go to war. They double-check their rifles, adjust their Kevlar vests, and line up in formation by the Loganstin Police armored van. "They're getting ready to storm the place," I say.

Wooden's voice booms again from outside, actually vibrating the windows. "You have thirty seconds!"

"Any good ideas?" Kent asks, a tremor in his voice.

A dozen SWAT team members move toward the front door. "This is your last warning," the chief of police says.

"Maybe the two of you should surrender," I say. "It's really me they're after."

"We're not leaving," Yvonne says.

The chief of police nods his head to the SWAT team. The dozen heavily armed men storm into the building.

"Okay, I guess this is it," I say, digging into my pocket. Pulling out the two remaining syringes of blue liquid, I remove the protective covers over the needles and promptly jam them into my thigh, emptying the contents into my bloodstream. With a rising sense of dread, I stare at the door of the apartment, waiting for the inevitable: SWAT team members with guns. "Calm down, Marvin," I whisper under my breath. I absorb my friends' fear and power courses through me. My senses are supercharged, and I can hear the SWAT team making its way up the stairs.

I glance out the window just as an orange plume explodes out of a sniper's rifle from across the street. Everything slows down. Way down. Grabbing Kent and Yvonne, I pull them away from the window a fraction of a second before a bullet shatters it.

There's a loud crash as the battering ram makes contact with the door. The door cracks, splinters, and is ripped off its hinges. The battering ram smashes through and hits me in the stomach. This makes tiny cracks appear in the head of the battering ram, which then spread through the hulking metal like glass shattering. The four SWAT team members holding it can only watch as it falls to the ground in chunks. They look at me, confused.

Time ticks slowly. Everything seems to be frozen. I wait for the men to move. We all look at each other, waiting for someone to do something. I grab the nearest man's rifle and squeeze, collapsing and twisting the metal barrel in my hand as easily as butter. In the hall, other members of the SWAT team pull their triggers. A series of bullets explode from the barrels in orange blossoms. I dodge them, and they pelt the walls and floor.

I move on the men, striking them in the chests, which sends three of them hurtling back through the air. They fly through the hall until they slam into the wall and crash to the floor. The others level their rifles at me again, but before they can pull the triggers, I knock them off their feet. One of the men smashes through the drywall.

The rest of the SWAT team, on the stairs, unleash a flurry of gunfire. The bullets are like giant raindrops that pour down on me. But everything happens so slowly—the bullets hang in the air as if crawling toward me. Some of them tear through plaster and wood, kicking up a storm of debris in the hallway.

I move toward the stairs, zipping there so fast that the SWAT team continues to fire at where I was just standing. Snatching the Kevlar vest of the man closest to me, I hoist him into the air and toss him at his teammates. He crashes into the others, sending them all careening down the stairs.

I grab two unconscious SWAT team members, one in each hand, and lug them into the apartment like I'm carrying bags of groceries. Yvonne and Kent clear out of my way. I set the two men down on the floor. "Take off your clothes," I say to my friends. I remove the SWAT team uniforms, leaving the men in their underwear, and toss the black paramilitary clothing at Yvonne and Kent's feet. "Hurry," I say. "We don't have much time."

My friends get undressed. Seeing Yvonne standing there in nothing but her underwear takes me aback. She blushes as she bends down to retrieve the clothing. "It's not polite to stare," she says.

Embarrassed, I look away, immediately sorry when my eyes land on Kent, who definitely doesn't look as good as Yvonne in his underwear. "Yeah, dude, it's not polite to stare," he says.

Yvonne and Kent adjust their outfits, which are a little big for them, but serviceable. I toss Kent a helmet. "Put this on."

He puts on the helmet, which helps conceal his melting face.

Sirens grow louder as more police cars arrive on the scene. "You should go now," I say, "before they regroup."

"What about you?" Yvonne asks.

Heading away from the window, I step out into the hall. A couple of the men moan and stir. I find one that's still unconscious, hoist him over my shoulder, and carry him down the stairs. Yvonne and Kent are in tow behind me. They struggle to move in the restrictive outfits, but they manage.

"I'm going to hang back until you two get safely away, and then I'll zip out of here," I say. "Let's meet up at home."

"Do you think it's safe there?" Yvonne asks.

"We'll hurry, collect only the necessities, and beat feet," I say. We reach the ground floor and sneak toward the front door, careful to stay out of sight.

"What're we supposed to do with him?" Kent asks, propping up the unconscious man.

"Get your teammate medical attention," I say, winking. "While they're attending to him, you guys sneak away."

Yvonne and Kent struggle to carry the man toward the front door. Yvonne glances back at me before stepping out into the daylight. They head toward the police barricade. A couple of police officers hurry out and help them lay the unconscious man down on a gurney, which paramedics lift into the back of an ambulance.

There's a flurry of activity surrounding the building. It's chaos. People run, holler, and argue. Chief Wooden screams at anyone within earshot and some who're not. As he surveys his underlings, he spots Yvonne and Kent. His suspicious eyes fix on them. He grabs the shirt of a nearby police officer and points my friends out, pushing the man in their direction.

The officer makes his way through the crowd, heading toward Yvonne and Kent.

Desperate to create a diversion, I run back into the building and bound up the stairs, snatching up a rifle. I run to the nearest window on the second floor. Using the butt of the gun, I shatter the glass, then point the barrel into the air and pull the trigger, releasing a stream of bullets harmlessly skyward. People below duck for cover, hiding behind vehicles. The police officer heading toward my friends momentarily forgets what he's doing and jumps behind an ambulance. Yvonne and Kent sneak away through the crowd. Managing to make their way down the street, they turn and disappear behind a rundown building.

Dropping the rifle on the ground, I turn around and see Mystic appear in a green cloud of smoke. "How'd you get in here?" I ask.

"I'm a bounder," she says.

I've never met a bounder before, and to be honest, I thought they were nothing more than an urban legend. Bounders can disappear and reappear anywhere their minds can imagine. They travel at the speed of thought.

Mystic peers out the window at the mayhem below. "It isn't easy living with regret."

"You were reading my mind again."

"Yes—I *overhead* what you told your friends about your father," she says. "When you get to my age, you look back at your life and cringe about decisions you made along the way. But there's nothing I can do about that now. I can't change the past." Mystic can't hide the sadness in her eyes.

Recognizing that there's not much left to say, I head toward the stairs.

"It would've been real easy for you to join the Core," Mystic says.

With my back to her, I say, "The price is too high."

"Be careful that your moral compass doesn't lead you into danger," Mystic says. "People like you seem to disappear in this city."

"Are you saying you're the one who'll make us disappear?"

"There are others out there far worse than us who have you in their crosshairs," she says. "I've going to give you one last piece of unsolicited advice—give that data sticker to Chief Wooden. He's an asshole, but he's an honest asshole."

I speed down the stairs and make my way out the front door, weaving through the barricade of police. Chaos swirls all around me as police officers scramble to reposition themselves for another offensive on the building.

I stop right in front of the chief of police, interrupting him in mid-bark. Startled, he staggers back. "What the hell!" he says. Recognition dawns on his face as he reaches for his sidearm. "Don't you move!"

I grab his wrist and stop him from pulling the handgun from the holster clipped to his belt. "You were right about the Core," I say. Before he has time to say or do anything, I place the data sticker in his open palm. He glances down at it, and by the time he looks up, I'm already gone.

TWENTY-NINE

One second I'm moving faster than the eye can see, the next I'm as immobile as a giant redwood, rooted in place by the overpass. I can't help but wonder whether or not there will be side effects from taking so much of Dr. Klaus's concoction. If something is too good to be true, then it usually is. I guess it's for the best I'm out of the stuff.

Yvonne and Kent are just making their way back. Kent unfastens the chin strap of the helmet and says, "Help me get this off." His face is spread across the inside of the visor like a bug that's met its demise on a windshield. I grab the helmet and yank, which nearly pulls Kent over. I yank again and manage to pull it off. His head expands and immediately hangs down in slabs. "That's better," he sighs. He doesn't even bother undressing, just oozes out of his clothing. "I don't think I could keep my body together for another second."

"Go pack whatever you can carry," I say. "We've got to get out of here."

"Where're we going to go?" Yvonne asks.

"I've got enough money to get a cheap hotel room for a week or two," Kent says.

Yvonne begins to remove the SWAT gear. "And after that?"

I shrug. "One thing at a time."

Kent hobbles into the concrete cave. "I'm gonna miss this place."

Yvonne finishes removing her gear and stands there a moment.

"I'm really sorry, Yvonne," I say.

"Marvin, we'll get through this together." She leans forward and plants a kiss on my mouth, then disappears inside.

I stand there a moment, smiling.

"I don't like finding my man kissing another woman," a voice says behind me. Eliza steps out from behind a pillar. She doesn't move toward me, just stands there at a distance.

"How'd you know I'd come here?" I ask.

"I always knew you lived here with Yvonne and Kent. Yes, I knew it was Yvonne who drugged Streak and that Kent and you were there with her."

"What do you want?"

"I'm just tying up loose ends," Eliza says. "You're kind of gullible, Marvin. Once you believed you were trying out for the Core, you were mine."

"But why kill Mercury?"

Eliza snarls as she says, "He'd grown soft and lazy. I can do a better job leading the Core."

"That's why you killed him? To be the leader of the Core?"

"You make it sound like I needed some other reason," she says, circling around me like a cat toying with a wounded mouse. "Darren could fly through the sun without getting a blister. So when I read in the paper about you saving that family, I knew what I was going to do. It was a no-brainer. I told Mercury that I was going public with everything I knew about his criminal activity. That was enough to get him to come after me. He couldn't take the chance that I'd reveal the Core's cozy relationship with organized crime. I mean, come on, Mercury a hero? He rates as one of the worst. He did it all and then some. He was rotten to the Core."

"You were the good guys."

"Dr. Klaus gave me your test results," she says. "When powers develop in most people, the level of power stays basically the same from day one to the day the person dies. But your powers are different. Apparently, your powers are increasing. You could've been the first Level 10 ever recorded."

"Could've?"

Bright light glows from her eyes as she says, "You're not going to live long enough for us to find out."

A burst of energy erupts from her eyes. I jump out of the way as the blast hits the ground where I was just standing. Zipping into the concrete cave, I speed down the corridor. I glance back and see Eliza's silhouette framed in the doorway. "Sorry, Marvin. I really did like you," she says. The next blast from her eyes makes a deafening noise as it strikes the concrete. She rotates her head as the energy beam shoots out of her eyes and burns through the walls, which burst into flame and melt like lava oozing from a volcano. The fire spreads, moving deeper into our home.

She's just visible behind the smoke and flames. She blows me a kiss and is gone.

Black smoke from the concrete burns my lungs. Coughing violently, I race off to find my friends. Yvonne and Kent are in the living room. Kent sticks his nose into the air, sniffing. "Do you guys smell something burning?" he asks.

"We've got to get out of here," I say. "There's a fire heading this way."

"A fire?" Kent says. "What's it burning?"

"The concrete."

"How is that possible?" Yvonne asks.

"Eliza," I say.

Running out of the living room, we see the blaze heading toward us. "The overpass will collapse," Yvonne says.

"The only way out is the crawl space," I say. "Come on." We race deeper into the concrete cave, putting as much distance between the blaze and ourselves as we can.

"Where are we going? The crawl space grate is in the kitchen," Kent says.

"The fire has spread past the kitchen," I tell him.

"Then how're we going to get into the crawl space?" Yvonne pants.

The corridor comes to an abrupt end. The slab of concrete over our heads angles down until it makes a perfect point with the floor. This is the farthest point of the concrete cave. Six inches of cement separate us from freedom. The road rests just above us. I walk as far as I can before I have to get down on my hands and knees and crawl on all fours. Yvonne and Kent follow my lead. The black smoke chokes us. It fills my nostrils and makes me retch. I stare at the stress point where the concrete comes together. The blaze is growing increasingly brighter as it moves toward us slowly and methodically, like a slasher from a horror movie stalking its teenage prey.

Pointing to the stress point, I say, "I'm pretty sure if a lot of pressure is applied to this point right there, it'll crumble."

Fear and apprehension are on my friends' faces. "That's your plan?" Kent stammers.

Pulling back my fist, I muster what's left of my strength from the blue concoction and throw a punch at the stress point. My hand lands with a deep thud, and I feel the vibrations from the impact traveling deep into the concrete. The initial punch doesn't do much, but that wasn't my intention. As I pummel the concrete again and again, striking it to a uniform beat, I hope Dr. Klaus's serum lasts long enough for this to work.

"Marvin, what are you doing?" Yvonne screams. I can barely hear her over the sound of my fist smacking the concrete. It's like a jackhammer. The area around us gets brighter as the fire moves closer. Kent and Yvonne gag and cough as the thick smoke closes around them.

I feel the concrete under my feet wobble as the repetitive force of my punches causes rhythmic waves. I steady myself and continue to pound my fist against the wall.

I hope the book *Strange Phenomenons Explained* was right about the seismic wave toppling the city's walls during the Battle of Jericho.

My friends try to cover their noses and mouths as they choke on the black smoke. The fire is nearly on top of us now. Looking at Yvonne and Kent, I shout, "Scream as loud as you can. Now!"

Chalk it up to fear, but my friends supply me with blood-curdling screams. Joining in their chorus, I yell at the top of my lungs. The shouts cause the concrete near me to crack. I feel the ground beneath my feet shift and wobble, like ripples caused by a rock being tossed into a calm and peaceful pond. The giant slabs of concrete begin to shift and crack. The stress point opens, revealing the crawl space below.

"Move it!" I yell, pushing Yvonne into it. She scurries forward on her belly. Kent pours himself in and slithers after her. I drop down and follow my friends. The heat from the fire burns the back of my legs. It nips at my heels as I hurry down the tiny space. My face sinks into Kent's gooey backside.

Crawling out of the passageway, I stand up in the utility corridor. I lead my friends to the rusty ladder. "Hurry! Move!" I climb up the ladder and out through the manhole cover. Breathing in deeply, I notice that the fresh night air has never felt so good.

We lie on the ground. "Is everyone okay?" I ask.

Yvonne coughs violently, but finally manages to catch her breath. "Yeah," she says.

"I'm okay … I think," Kent coughs.

The concrete lets out a final scream. The overpass support columns twist and buckle. A section of the bridge dislodges, plummeting to the freeway below and revealing the moon on the horizon. A mountain of concrete rains down. It's the loudest noise I've ever heard. The wreckage is extensive. Chunks of concrete are strewn about. Steel beams, twisted and bent, stick out of the rubble. Smoke rises out of the debris. From what I can see, there are a dozen or so vehicles crushed underneath the concrete and metal, and another hundred vehicles jammed up in either direction, with many of the drivers jumping out to help dig people out of the mangled vehicles.

An entire section of the overpass is missing, and a car dangles over the side with people trapped inside. "We've got to help," I say, leaping up. I'm tired. There are twinges of pain in my legs, but I force myself to ignore it. Whatever I'm going to do, I've got to do it fast, because I'm going to crash soon.

Joining a handful of people, I rush over to the red sedan hanging over the edge, awed by the gaping hole in the bridge. I'm jarred back to reality by a man with gray hair wearing a business suit who's yelling, "Grab it before it falls!"

With about ten other men, I take hold of the car's back end and hold on for dear life. Through the rear window, we see a woman scrambling from the driver's seat into the backseat, where a small boy is fastened into a car seat. The three-year-old boy has big tears running down his chubby cheeks.

"On the count of three," the gray-haired man says, "pull as hard as you can!" I didn't notice before, but Yvonne is standing next to me, holding on to the car. "One. Two. Three!"

I pull with all my might. When I don't feel the car budge, I redouble my efforts. The men and Yvonne grunt and curse as they struggle to pull the sedan to safety, but the vehicle doesn't move a single inch. The woman in the car frantically unbuckles her son, who isn't making it easy for her. He flails his arms and kicks his feet, deathly afraid.

"Pull harder!" someone screams.

I hear a popping noise, and one of the men falls to one knee, grimacing in pain. He scoots out of the way and Kent takes his place, pulling hard, which stretches his arms unnaturally long, like rubber bands.

"It's not working!" Yvonne yells.

There's a sound of metal scraping against concrete, and for

a split second I think we're making progress, but instead of the car being pulled back, it slides a few inches forward, dangling even farther over the edge. Clutching her son, the mother tries to roll down the back window. The car tilts forward, its hood pointing down as if inspecting the hundred-foot drop.

"Someone do something!" a woman screams from behind us.

The sedan lurches forward. Three men run up and try to open the back doors, but they're jammed. The car teeters, and as it settles, it begins to slide forward.

"Let go! Let go of the car or you'll be pulled down with it!" someone screams.

Everyone lets go and jumps back, helplessly watching as the mother and son start to go over the edge. I'm the only one still hanging on. "I will not let go!" I scream. I'm pulled forward as the car slips farther over. The tips of my sneakers protrude over the ledge. The woman sobs as she clutches her son to her chest.

I dig my heels into the ground and say, "I will not let this happen!"

Everything goes silent. I don't hear the mother scream, nor her son cry. I don't hear the cries for help of the people trapped inside the rubble. I don't hear my friends shouting my name. I don't even hear the rustling of the wind as it whispers across the landscape. The only thing I hear is the beating of my heart.

Standing at the very edge, I clutch the back of the car. I'm afraid if I move, I'll forfeit what remains of my power and the car will slip from my grip. The gray-haired man walks over and peers over the ledge. The woman in the car opens her eyes and stares at me, confusion on her face.

"Can you pull the car back up?" the gray-haired man asks.

I step back, and the car moves with me. I pull it back up onto the overpass, stopping when it's a safe distance from the edge.

A group of men rush over and pry open the back door, helping the woman and the small boy out. The woman runs toward me, still clutching her son. "Oh, thank you! Thank you!" she says. She wraps her free arm around me and gives me a hug. Her tears of joy wet my cheeks. "You saved our lives," she says. "Thank you."

"You're welcome," I say, smiling.

The crowd of people breaks out in applause. Yvonne gives me a warm smile, and the sight of her standing there amid the rubble and debris under the blue sky makes me feel like I can soar.

"Way to go!" someone says.

"What's your name?" a lady asks.

"Marvin," Kent says, draping his arm around my shoulder. "My best friend."

The gray-haired man points. "They need help."

My friends and I stand at the edge and look down at the wreckage below. People are still scurrying about, digging others out of the rubble. "Let's get down there," I say.

We all run down the embankment and race to the nearest pile of rubble. People are trying to move jagged blocks of concrete away from a truck. A man is trapped inside. The people stand aside as I begin heaving enormous pieces of concrete. I can hear them say, in hushed tones, that I'm a hero. Once I've moved the heaviest debris, the people clear the rubble and help the man out of the truck, and I move on to another buried car.

After disrobing, Kent dissolves and oozes into the rubble.

He looks like a stream of thick, fleshy liquid. He's gone for a few moments but then his torso reappears, shaping back into its normal form. The bottom half of his body remains in the rubble, like he's waist-deep in water. He points down and I hear him tell people who've gather around, "There's a man buried under there." Following his directions, people begin clearing away the wreckage. Kent moves on to another pile, again melting into the remains of the overpass.

Yvonne kneels next to a man who's sprawled out on the ground. He has a nasty cut on his forehead and, judging by the unnatural position of his arm, a few broken bones. Yvonne rests her hand gently on his forehead and closes her eyes. The man's face relaxes and he stops moaning in agony.

The sound of sirens approaches in the distance. I look up and see a handful of ambulances and police cars driving along the shoulder of the road toward us. Kent lumbers over to me, buttoning up his pants. "We better get outta here."

"No. There are still people trapped."

"But what about the cops?" he asks.

"We'll deal with that once we're done," I say, going back to work.

"Okay." He smiles. "You're the boss."

That's when I hear a stern voice behind me say, "I think you've done enough here." Sling and Rocket are standing on top of a pile of rubble. "You three are coming with us."

Just at that moment, I feel the blackness come up behind me, snaring me like a trap. I lose all strength and drop to my knees.

"Marvin?!" Yvonne screams.

I fall forward onto the ground. Everything goes black.

THIRTY

My eyes flutter open. A rich darkness blankets me. Pushing myself up, I look around. I immediately recognize that I'm in Eliza's Roisin shrine. An empty shrine. The queen-size bed I'm in is the softest thing I've ever lain on. An IV drip attached to a metal roller rests by the side of the bed.

I swing my feet off the bed and plant them on the floor. I stand up and wish I hadn't. I'm lightheaded and topple back onto the bed. My butt sinks into the down comforter.

"You're up," Yvonne says, rushing to my side. She takes my hand in hers. "How do you feel?"

The room is spinning. "I'm dizzy," I say.

She squeezes my hand and says, "I'm so glad you're awake."

"How long have I been out?" When she doesn't answer, I open my eyes and fix them on her. "Yvonne?"

She blinks repeatedly, as if trying to hold the waterworks back. "A month."

"Come again?"

"You've been out for a month."

"And we're at Eliza's safe house?"

"After the ruckus, this place went back to being forgotten about."

"What happened after I blacked out?" I ask. "I remember Sling and Rocket, but that's it."

"Kent and I made a deal that we can't tell you about it until we're both here," she says.

"Why?"

"You'll just have to wait," Yvonne says.

"Where's Kent?"

"He's out rustling up some food." Yvonne removes the tape covering the IV syringe and gently pulls the needle out of my arm. "Are you hungry?"

"Yeah," I say. My stomach growls, as if seconding that statement.

Yvonne coils up the tubing. "You've been living on a liquid diet for a month, so I imagine you could use some real food."

Motioning to the IV, I say, "Where did you get that?"

"I borrowed it from an emergency room," she says.

I poke the nearly full bag of liquid hanging from the IV stand and say, "What have you been pumping into me?"

"Everything a growing boy needs," Yvonne says. "A cocktail of saline, vitamins, and protein."

"Sounds delicious."

"You had us pretty scared, Marvin," she says. "We didn't think it was safe taking you to the hospital. Kent and I did the best we could on our own."

Rubbing my arm where the needle was removed, I say, "I'm alive, so that says something."

"It was touch-and-go there for a bit." Her body trembles and she begins to sob uncontrollably. I pull her to me and hold her. She recoils and pounds her fists against my chest. "Don't you ever do that again! Do you hear me?! Never again!"

I give her my best reassuring smile and say, "I promise." She wipes the tears from her eyes. "So you missed me, huh?"

She laughs despite herself. "Don't get a big head. I just didn't want to be left alone with Kent, that's all."

As if speaking his name summoned him, Kent strolls into the room. "Dude, you're up!" He falls on top of me. His soft body spreads out and blankets me.

Struggling, I manage to move my head out from under his flesh. "It's good to see you too, Kent," I croak.

"You're going to suffocate him," Yvonne says, peeling him off me.

"When did he wake up?"

"Just now."

"You didn't tell him yet, did you?" he asks.

"No. I waited for you."

"Dude, we're famous."

"What?" I say.

"We're like totally famous."

Yvonne nods and says, "It's true."

"How's that?"

"Do you remember what happened at the overpass?" Kent asks.

"Not really."

Kent rubs his hands together gleefully. "Dude, this is so cool. So Rocket and Sling arrive on the scene. They start posturing like peacocks and threatening us."

"But then all the normies we helped came rushing over," Yvonne says. "They surrounded Rocket and Sling and screamed at them that we were the good guys."

"That lady you saved in the car?" Kent says. "She runs over holding her kid and yells at them. She tells them we're heroes, how you saved her and her son. They looked like scolded children. And so they just took off. Up and bailed."

"And we grabbed you and got out of there," Yvonne says. "We bounced around for a bit but finally landed here."

"Show him the press conference," Yvonne says.

"Yeah, okay," Kent says, jumping up. He inserts a DVD into a small television and presses *play*. The screen is blue at first, but flickers as a recording of a news broadcast begins to play. A female news anchor sits at her desk. She presses her fingers to the concealed earpiece in her ear and listens before finally saying, "We will take you now to Mystic's press conference, already in progress."

The image on the television cuts to a small stage where Mystic stands behind a podium. Chief of Police Wooden stands at her side. She looks down at her prepared remarks and reads, sounding stifled and uncomfortable. "I'm here to set the record straight regarding the events of the last three weeks."

"When was this recorded?" I ask.

"About four days after you turned into a vegetable," Kent says. "Now shoosh! You're going to miss the best part."

Mystic looks up from her statement and stares directly into the camera. "Chief of Police Wooden and I want to make it crystal clear to the citizens of Loganstin and all the viewers around the world: Eliza Todd, a.k.a. Roisin, was the lone culprit in orchestrating the murder of Lieutenant

Mercury, as the footage anonymously given to the police chief shows." She stares at the camera for a beat, as if letting her words sink in to the millions of viewers listening to the broadcast. "Marvin Maywood, Yvonne McCalmon, and Kent Patterson had nothing to do with the planning of this heinous and ghastly crime. These three young, extraordinary IWPs were thrust into a plot and have been wrongly implicated. As demonstrated the other day, at the collapse of the overpass, they are heroes. And my deepest desire is that the three of them will one day think of me as a friend."

Kent nudges me in the ribs with a soft elbow. "Can you believe it?"

"No. No, I can't," I mutter.

Mystic looks back down at her notes and continues to read. "It has also come to light that some members of the Core were engaged in illegal activities. As the new leader of the Core, I am working closely with local law enforcement to investigate these allegations, as well as bring about the swift capture of Eliza Todd. It is believed that she has fled Loganstin. We are asking for the public's help. If anyone has any information as to her whereabouts, please contact the Loganstin Police Department. Thank you."

Mystic and the chief of police make a hasty exit from the stage, leaving behind a flurry of questions from members of the press.

Kent stops the recording and turns off the television. "What do you think?" he asks.

"I ... I don't know," I say.

"We're off the hook," Yvonne says.

"Can you believe it?" Kent says. "They're calling us heroes."

"Who is?"

"Our adoring public."

"Heroes," I say, liking the sound of it.

My friends look at each other, silently petitioning one another with raised eyebrows. "You say it," Kent says to Yvonne.

She turns to me, smiles, and says, "We've got something to tell you."

Kent has a big cheesy grin plastered on his face.

"What?" I ask.

"We like being heroes," Kent says.

EPILOGUE

The Midtown Café breakfast crowd has thinned out. Waitresses sit at the counter, tallying their receipts and counting out their tips. The new busboy, Ben, scurries around cleaning off the tables. I've met Ben a couple times now, and he seems like a nice-enough guy.

He spots me and nods his head. "Hey, Marvin. Gus is in his office."

I knock on the office door.

"Come in," Gus calls from the other side.

I open the door and peer in. Gus looks up from punching in numbers on a calculator. He leans back in his chair.

"So?" he says.

I smile and say, "We're in." I shut the office and take a seat across the desk from him.

He stares at me for a few moments before slapping his hands down on his desk. "Great!"

"You knew what I was going to say, didn't you?"

"The second you stepped through the door," he says.

When I first came in after all the excitement and asked Gus for my job back, he told me that he was an IWP too. A dirty, at that. He confessed that since he's a mind reader, he knew all about me and my friends. When I asked why he never mentioned my powers, he explained that he was waiting for me to come to him. It was my secret, he said, and secrets should be shared, not stolen. Then he told me that Yvonne and I couldn't have our old jobs back anyway. We're famous now, and if word got out that we worked here, it would attract too much attention. Every two-bit thug wanting to make a name for himself would come gunning for us.

Today, Gus reaches into his hip pocket to retrieve his wallet, pulls out some bills, and slides them across the desk to me. "Here's a little something to help you get by."

"I don't want to take your money if I don't work for it," I say.

"You are working for it," he says.

"You know what I mean, Gus."

"Marvin, you and your friends are going to help me way more this way than you ever could by cleaning up dishes," he says. "I've done things in my past that I'm not proud of—and what we're planning to do together is something I have to do. I *have* to." He flashes me a warm smile. "So please take the money."

I reach out and take it.

"Good." Gus opens a desk drawer, pulls out a notepad, and flips through the pages. "I've got a lead on a real dirt bag who's trying to buy plutonium to make a dirty bomb." He rips out the piece of paper and hands it to me. "Are you hungry?"

"Always."

He pushes back from the desk and stands up. "Then let's go get you something to eat."

It never ceases to amaze me how unpredictable life is. A month ago, I was Public Enemy No. 1, and now I'm a hero. I think there are two types of people—those who view life's uncertainty with dread and fear, and those who recognize that this unpredictably is what makes life worth living. If we could see every twist and turn in the road, what would be the point of taking the journey? I, for one, believe life's unpredictability ushers in more joy than pain. When times are bad—and my friends and I have had our fair share—I never give up hope that things will eventually change for the better. It can't always be bad, and the trick is to hang in there until it turns around. It takes the sour to make the good all that much sweeter.

Yvonne, Kent, and I—and now Gus—are a family, a strange and sometimes dysfunctional family, but a family nonetheless. I know that no matter what comes our way, we'll face the challenge together.

Gus and I walk out of the office. As he shuts the door behind us, a troubling thought begins to form in my head, but I quickly think of something else. I don't want him reading that thought.

THE END

Photo by Jamie Reese

About the Author

Christopher E. Long's comic book writing has been published by Marvel Comics, IDW Publishing, Boom! Studios, and Image Comics. He was born in Seattle, Washington, raised in North Logan, Utah, and currently lives in Southern California with his wife and son. Visit him online at www.christopherelong.com.